HUSTLE

HUSTLE
Johnny Boateng

James Lorimer & Company Ltd., Publishers
Toronto

James Lorimer & Company Ltd., Publishers acknowledges the support of the Ontario Arts Council. We acknowledge the financial support of the Government of Canada through the Canada Book Fund for our publishing activities. We acknowledge the support of the Canada Council for the Arts which last year invested $24.3 million in writing and publishing throughout Canada. We acknowledge the Government of Ontario through the Ontario Media Development Corporation's Ontario Book Initiative.

Cover design: Meredith Bangay
Cover image: Shutterstock

Library and Archives Canada Cataloguing in Publication

Boateng, Johnny, author
        Hustle / Johnny Boateng.

(Sports stories)
Issued in print and electronic formats.
ISBN 978-1-4594-0604-9 (pbk.).--ISBN 978-1-4594-0605-6 (bound).--
ISBN 978-1-4594-0606-3 (epub)

        I. Title. II. Series: Sports stories (Toronto, Ont.)

PS8603.O27H87 2014   jC813'.6   C2013-906823-6
C2013-906824-4

James Lorimer & Company Ltd.,   Distributed in the United States by:
Publishers   Orca Book Publishers
317 Adelaide Street West, Suite 1002   P.O. Box 468
Toronto, ON, Canada   Custer, WA USA
M5V 1P9   98240-0468
www.lorimer.ca

Printed and bound in Canada.
Manufactured by Friesens Corporation in Altona, Manitoba, Canada in March 2014.
Job #201006

To all the young boys and girls chasing their dreams.
Where there is a will there is always a way.

CONTENTS

1 BETTER THAN YOU

Pamp! Pamp! Fourteen-year-old Johnny Huttle pounded a tattered basketball into the pavement of the run-down playground. Focused on the hoop in front of him, he didn't notice the sweat dripping down his forehead and pooling just below his chin. He twirled the basketball in his hands. The ball was worn all the way down to its seams, just the way he liked it. He'd been practicing for hours, but he couldn't quit. Not yet.

"Get up, kid! This one is for the game," he coached himself.

His muscles tensed as he gripped the ball. He took off running, counting down the seconds in his head as he sprinted toward the hoop.

"7 . . . 6 . . . 5 . . ." He dribbled the ball behind his back, spun left and then spun right.

"4 . . . 3 . . . 2 . . . 1 . . ." About a metre in front of the hoop, he jumped. He cocked the ball back as he soared through the air. But as he reached the rim, he realized he wasn't quite high enough.

Thud! The ball stuck to the front of the rim like a magnet. Johnny's arm jerked and he fell backward fast. Johnny began to panic when he realized his legs weren't where they were supposed to be.

Smack! Johnny landed on his back. He lay on the pavement in a crumpled heap. Then he rolled onto his side and groaned. He'd worked hard all summer and he still couldn't slam dunk the basketball every time he tried.

Suddenly, the sound of sneakers on the pavement disturbed Johnny's thoughts.

"Still trying to dunk, huh?" Rex King said, picking up the basketball. Rex twirled the ball on his finger and then jumped toward the hoop. He soared high above the rim. He stretched his arms and flushed the basketball through the rim.

"That's way too easy for you," Johnny said, shaking his head in disbelief. Rex was the only fifteen-year-old Johnny knew who could slam dunk a basketball that easily. Really tall, with light skin and curly golden hair, Rex already looked like an NBA star.

"All you have to do is jump. It's easy," Rex said.

"Yeah, I know, I was dunking everything before you got here," Johnny lied. "Why weren't you at school today?" He grabbed the ball away from Rex.

"Took the day off," Rex smirked.

"Don't let Coach Tanaka find out you're taking holidays," Johnny said, dribbling the ball behind his back.

"Don't worry about me, Hustle," Rex said and snatched back the ball.

Hustle. Rex had given Johnny that nickname years ago. Just like any nickname Rex gave anyone, it stuck.

"Give me my ball back. Can't you see I'm practicing?" Johnny took the ball from Rex and dribbled it in a figure-eight between his legs.

"Practice? For what?" Rex grumbled as he removed his sweatshirt.

"The Penticton Classic tournament starts tomorrow. There could be scouts there. If Coach lets me play, I want to be sharp." Johnny leaped into the air and shot the ball toward the hoop.

KA-CHING! His jump shot hit the bottom of the chain mesh.

"I've been perfecting that jump shot all summer long, baby. I'm telling you, I'm nice, man. I'm ready!" Johnny shouted, holding his hand in the air with a perfect follow-through.

"Child, please!" Rex laughed, retrieving the ball. "Just get me the ball. You know I'll carry us. I'm the one with the skills to pay the bills, baby." Rex tossed the ball back to Johnny.

"Yeah, right." The problem was, Rex was right. It wasn't fair. Rex barely practiced but he was always on top of his game.

"You know I got your game in my back pocket!" Rex taunted as he paced back and forth.

"That's it! Game up to eleven. Possession right away. Call your own fouls," Johnny challenged, pounding the ball into the pavement.

"Your court, your rules, bro. Check up, chump." Rex replied.

Johnny fired the ball at Rex and crouched, ready to play one-on-one.

Rex drove to the hoop and dipped his shoulder into Johnny's chest. The blow knocked Johnny onto the pavement. Rex finished the drive with a thunderous two-handed slam dunk.

"That's a foul on you, man!" Johnny yelled, jumping to his feet.

"This is street ball. You better man up, Hustle," Rex barked back.

Johnny got back into his defensive stance. Rex missed a long shot and Johnny grabbed the rebound.

"See! You do miss!" Johnny shouted.

"Rarely."

On offence, Johnny made a quick move and scored with his jump shot. On the next play, he drove to the hoop, but Rex was there to block his shot.

"Get that weak shot out of here, Hustle! Not in my house!" Rex shouted. They played for hours. Rex won every game. It seemed the harder Johnny played, the better Rex became.

"Let's play one last game," Johnny said.

"Fine. You're just going to lose anyway," Rex said.

The two boys continued their battle. Johnny fouled Rex hard. Rex lost his balance and went flying face-first to the ground. Before Johnny could blink, Rex was back up on his feet.

"That's a foul. You just can't take it, can ya?" Rex flicked the ball back to Johnny.

"I'm so sick of your mouth," Johnny muttered.

"So, shut me up. Stop me. But you know you can't beat me. Nobody can," Rex said, goading Johnny into action.

Johnny started pushing Rex, elbowing him and slapping at the ball. He'd show Rex that he couldn't beat him.

As Johnny reached to slap the ball away, Rex dodged him with a nice dribble move. The ball bounced off the ground like lightning with each move Rex made.

"Stop reaching or I'm teaching!" Rex warned. Johnny stuck Rex in the side with his forearm. Rex slapped his arm away. "Get off me, Hustle."

It began to rain, and the boys' feet slipped on the pavement. But they kept playing.

"I'm going up to the fifteenth floor. You stay in the lobby, Hustle."

"Not this time, Rex."

In a flurry, Rex made several dribble moves and fakes, and then headed hard to the hoop. The ball stuck to his right hand like it was glued there. Johnny moved to cut him off, but Rex made another move to dodge him. The move threw Johnny off balance and he stumbled.

Rex jumped up and Johnny jumped with him. They were above the rim. Johnny had never jumped so high before. He raised his right hand in the air to block the shot, but Rex soared even higher and turned his back to the net in mid-air.

Slam! Rex threw down a monstrous reverse slam dunk. He hung on the rim as Johnny returned to the ground. Rex wrapped his legs around Johnny's neck.

"Get off me!" Johnny said, pushing Rex's legs off his shoulders.

"Whoo! Yeah, baby! That's game!" Rex exclaimed.

Johnny grabbed the basketball. Rex danced in the middle of the court. He had his hands to the sky like he was accepting praise from God. Johnny thought about throwing the ball at Rex. But even if the ball hit Rex square in the back, Rex probably wouldn't flinch.

"Walk like a cham-PION, talk like a cham-PION. I am a cham-PION!" Rex sang at the top of his lungs as he danced. Johnny cringed each time Rex sang "-PION!"

Then, as if nothing had happened, Rex picked up his Lakers sweatshirt and pulled the hood over his face.

"Good game, man," Rex said, extending a hand for Johnny to shake.

"Jerk!" Johnny said bitterly.

Rex grabbed Johnny and hugged him.

"Go home!" Johnny pushed Rex back.

"Seriously, man, good game," Rex said, trying to sound sincere.

Johnny slammed the ball into the pavement. He hated losing to Rex.

"It's getting dark. I'm going home." Johnny slipped on his Hill Academy Knights sweatshirt.

"Yeah, all right. So what are we having for dinner?" Rex asked, as the boys made their way off the court.

"Probably Jaloff rice and goat meat tonight," Johnny said.

"Sweet, I'm starving," Rex said.

POP! POP! POP! Suddenly, blasts that sounded like giant balloons exploding echoed in the sky.

VROOM! The roar of a car engine rumbled nearby. The car was getting closer.

"C'mon, Hustle, let's go!" Rex shouted

Rex grabbed Johnny by the arm. Ducking low, the boys sprinted off the court.

"The hide out!" Johnny yelled.

"You know it!" Rex shouted back.

The boys leaped a fence and darted through alleyways. They cut through some bushes and stopped at an old shed beside a boarded-up house. Rex arrived first. He held the shed door open for Johnny.

"Hurry up!" Rex said urgently.

POP! POP! POP! More blasts sounded in the sky.

"Did you see who was blasting?" Johnny asked once he was inside, gasping to catch his breath.

"Nope. Could have been anyone." Rex closed the shed door.

"Let's just wait here a bit."

"It's always like this," Rex said, settling in.

"I know. Everyone wants to act hard. When I get to the NBA, I'm going to clean up this whole neighbourhood," Johnny said.

"How are you going to do that, Hustle?" Rex asked. "Make the NBA?"

"No, how are you going to clean the 'hood up?"

"What? That's the easy part. I'll be in the NBA, which means I'll be paid for real. We're talking serious cash. I can hire a task force or a secret agent or something."

"You mean hire a snitch."

"No, I'll hire someone who will arrest all the dealers and stop the thugs from shooting people," Johnny explained.

"That's a snitch, Hustle."

"Do you even know what a snitch is?"

"Stop trying to be smart. So," Rex said, poking his head out from the shed, "you gonna ask out Tracy Melrose, or what?"

Johnny shrugged his shoulders. "Just let me do my thing. Why do you care so much anyway?"

"I don't. But if you ask me, you should be going for Amy Stackhouse. She's cool."

"I didn't ask you."

Johnny thought about it. Amy Stackhouse was the type of girl who was more concerned with doing well in school and playing basketball than with dating guys. Amy Stackhouse wasn't nearly as popular as Tracy Melrose.

"You think Amy's hotter than Tracy?" Johnny asked, already knowing the answer.

"Don't be stupid, Hustle. No girl is hotter than Tracy. But you don't want Tracy, man, trust me. She's not your type," Rex said, laughing.

"What's my type, then, Mr. Love Doctor?" Johnny asked.

"Not her." Rex stood up and put his hood back on. "Hey, I think we can make it to your place."

"All right, follow me," Johnny said. "I know a short cut."

2 OVER A GIRL

Smush, smush, smush. Johnny raced through a soggy football field toward the Hill Academy. A large charter bus roared to life in the parking lot as he got there.

Coach Tanaka stood in front of the bus, staring at his wristwatch. "You know, Johnny, most of the battle toward being successful is showing up on time," he said.

"Sorry, Coach," Johnny said, catching his breath.

"Get settled in." Coach Tanaka patted Johnny on the back as he climbed aboard.

"Hustle! You made it!" Rex yelled from the back of the bus.

Johnny cracked a smile, but it turned to a frown as he realized Rex hadn't saved him a seat. Rex was sitting with Tracy Melrose.

Tracy had long, golden-blond hair and big, blue eyes. She wore makeup and her skin was always tanned, even in the winter. Johnny tried to avoid staring at Tracy, but he couldn't help it.

Johnny tossed his bags into an empty seat at the

front of the bus. He plopped down, removed a comb from his backpack and quickly picked his mini-afro.

A Filipino boy dressed in hipster clothes sat down right beside him.

"Looks like it's me and you, bro, riding up front," Xandro Santos said, polishing the lenses of his large, dark-rimmed glasses.

"Looks like, bro," Johnny replied, smiling. Johnny slid the comb into his pocket and placed his arm around Xandro. They were the only two fourteen-year-olds to make Hill Academy's Junior Varsity team.

"Why are you polishing those lenses? You don't need glasses, man," Johnny said smirking.

"You know my style, Hustle." Xandro offered Johnny a fist bump.

A portly bus driver took his seat and put the bus into gear. In a few short minutes, they were roaring down the highway. In just over five hours they would be in Penticton.

The bus rolled on along the Trans-Canada Highway through glacier-filled mountain passes. Johnny tried his best to focus on the upcoming games. He was hoping all his practice would pay off. He sat back in his seat and imagined himself playing like a superstar, with thousands of fans cheering and chanting his name in the stands. A smile crept across his face.

The daydream was interrupted by roars of laughter and Tracy's voice. Rex and the other Grade Tens on the team were cracking jokes at the back of the bus.

Xandro nudged Johnny and leaned in close. "Look at Rex back there, trying to be a stud. I heard he snuck some booze on the bus," Xandro whispered.

Johnny shrugged his shoulders, but he really hoped Xandro was wrong.

Finally, the bus pulled into the parking lot of the Glenwood Hotel in Penticton. Aside from the silhouettes of some Victorian-style houses, not much could be seen of the small town.

As they filed off the bus, Coach Tanaka assigned rooms to the players. Johnny was rooming with Xandro.

Rex and Tracy exited the bus last, still joking around. Tracy was wearing Rex's Academy sweatshirt. Johnny thought Rex was acting like he was drunk, but couldn't tell if he really was.

There was a tap on Johnny's shoulder. "Hi, John." It was Amy Stackhouse, smiling and clutching a basketball under her arm.

"Hey, Amy," Johnny said, unable to take his eyes off Tracy and Rex. He watched as Tracy gave Rex a huge hug. Then she and Amy headed off to their room.

When Johnny and Xandro got to their room, Xandro called dibs on first shower, first bathroom privileges, control of the TV and everything else he could think of to call dibs on. Johnny didn't care, his mind was racing. *Had Rex really been drinking? Had Tracy?*

Johnny had just removed his math book from his

backpack when — *RAP! RAP!* — two knocks rattled the door.

"I'll go see who it is," Xandro said jumping out of bed.

RAP! RAP! Two more knocks.

"Who is out there trying to sound like the police?" Johnny called.

It was Rex. With him was Donny Charleston, the team's starting centre. Donny's curly, brown hair went down to his shoulders. He was so tall, he had to duck his head to walk through the door.

Rex shoved Xandro aside, knocking him to the ground.

"Hey, leave Xandro alone, man," Johnny said to Rex, his head still in his math book. "What do you guys want anyways?"

"We just came to visit you rooks," Donny said.

"I see you got your sweater back, Rex. You smell like a chick. And, Donny, you stink like booze," Johnny muttered.

Donny smelled his shirt and then sniffed Rex. "You can smell that?" Donny asked.

"From a mile away," Johnny answered.

Donny sniffed Rex again. "You do smell like a chick, bro." he said.

Rex ignored Donny. "Is that all you're going to do all night, Hustle? Be bitter and study?" Rex asked.

"I'm not bitter," Johnny lied.

"So you sat up front because you wanted to, right?" Donny joked.

"Shut up, Donny!" Johnny snapped.

"You shut up, bitter man," Donny snapped back.

"Donny, chill," Rex ordered. "Hustle, put the books away. We're going out."

Xandro jumped to his feet and started dancing. He paused in a b-boy stance. "Where are we going?"

Johnny laughed at Xandro's moves. Xandro was an awesome dancer.

But Rex wasn't impressed. "*You're* not going any-where." Rex shoved Xandro down to the ground again.

"It's past curfew and we have three games tomor-row," Johnny said.

"I told you he didn't have the stones to come out," Donny said to Rex.

"He's coming," Rex said confidently.

Johnny really didn't want to go. If they were caught, Coach Tanaka would probably bench them. They could even be suspended from school. But Johnny put on his Academy Knights team sweater. He had to go. Rex was his friend.

"You ready?" Rex asked, placing his arm around Johnny.

Johnny nodded. "Where are we going?" Johnny asked.

"Just follow," Rex said.

Johnny, Donny and Rex moved through the streets

of Penticton. Rex and Donny ran up the sidewalks and jumped over fences. They jumped on picnic tables and tried to talk to everyone they saw. Johnny felt for certain that someone would call the police.

"Let's go back," Johnny suggested.

"We're just going to grab something from the gas station first," Rex said.

Donny and Rex ran into a gas station while Johnny waited outside.

Moments later, Rex and Donny burst out of the gas station doors.

"Run!" Rex shouted as they ran past and headed off in different directions.

Johnny didn't hesitate. He turned and started sprinting. He could hear the gas station clerk yelling after them, but he didn't turn around.

Pat, pat, pat. Johnny could hear footsteps gaining on him. He turned around to see the store clerk sprinting after him.

"Wait till I catch you!" the store clerk shouted.

Johnny quickened his pace. He ran as if his life depended on it.

"I didn't do anything!" Johnny yelled back.

"Tell that to the police," the clerk shouted.

"It wasn't me!" Johnny shouted.

But the clerk continued to chase him. Johnny had no idea where to go or where to hide. He kept running and cutting through yards, trying to lose the clerk.

He could run forever if he had to.

After a long while, Johnny took a quick look behind him. He didn't know when the clerk had given up the chase, but the man was nowhere in sight.

Johnny looked around. Penticton was different from his neighbourhood in Vancouver where he knew every street, every block. Johnny was lost. He began to regret leaving the hotel.

For what seemed like hours, Johnny tried to retrace his steps, looking to find his way back to the hotel. It was hopeless because at night everything looked the same to him.

Johnny plopped down on the sidewalk. He was exhausted and upset that Rex and Donny had got him into such a mess.

Then he heard Rex calling his name. "Hustle!"

Johnny sighed heavily. Hearing Rex's voice was like sweet music to his tired ears.

Rex jogged over. "I've been looking for you, man. Have some chips," Rex offered, tilting a large bag toward Johnny. Johnny took a handful of chips and shoved them into his mouth.

"That crazy gas jockey tried to arrest me for those chips," Johnny said, trying to hide how relieved he was to see Rex.

"Yeah, something was wrong with that dude," Rex joked.

"Yeah, he hates being ripped off!" Johnny snapped.

"Relax, Hustle. It's just a bag of chips. Come on, I know the way back to the hotel," Rex said.

"Thank goodness," Johnny said, letting his relief show. "Where's Donny?"

"He got tired and went back to his room. I told him I'd find you. Do you know what time it is? I've been looking for you for hours," Rex said.

Rex placed his arm around Johnny and ruffled his hand through Johnny's afro.

Johnny could see that Rex had been worried about him. Stealing the chips was a stupid prank, but Rex hadn't gone back to the hotel until he knew Johnny was safe. "Thanks, bro," Johnny said.

"You know I got your back," Rex replied.

They sneaked back into their rooms, but Johnny was still wired from the chase and the hours of wandering. His heart was still thumping hard in his chest and his legs felt wobbly.

He checked the answering machine to see if his parents had called. His mother had left a message wishing him good luck. There was another message after that one. Johnny fumbled with the phone and played it. His heart thumped hard in his chest when he heard Tracy's voice. But his excitement quickly turned to dismay. Tracy was asking Rex why he hadn't met up with her. It was clear that she had called Johnny's room by mistake.

Johnny erased the message and jumped into his bed.

He closed his eyes and tried to sleep, but he couldn't. He tossed and turned in his bed. Rex was suddenly a mystery that Johnny couldn't figure out. He treated Johnny like a kid in front of the team — in front of Tracy. But instead of meeting up with Tracy, Rex got Johnny to come along on his stupid heist from the gas station. Johnny's mind started racing. Maybe Rex had planned to meet up with Tracy, but couldn't because he had felt responsible for Johnny getting lost? Johnny wondered if Rex would throw away their friendship over a girl. If the girl was Tracy, Johnny wondered if he would do it himself.

3 STEPPING UP

Johnny didn't say a word to any of his teammates at breakfast or on the bus ride to the Penticton gym. He couldn't stop thinking about Rex and Tracy.

Johnny hadn't yet earned a spot in the starting five. He started the first game on the bench, watching his team. Johnny could see that the Hill Academy Knights were much stronger and faster than the Penticton Rangers. But his team was playing sloppy and the game was close.

Coach Tanaka paced back and forth along the sideline. "We should be up by twenty!" he said, scratching his bald head.

Johnny watched the game closely. He looked for areas on the court where he could make plays when he got his chance to play.

Rex was spectacular. Rex shot three-point baskets on four straight plays. He shot the last one from just inside the half-court line. That one hit nothing but net. The crowd gasped in admiration.

Johnny looked around and noticed that there wasn't an empty seat in the gym, everyone was there to watch Rex put on a show. He was anxious to show the large crowd what he could do.

Late in the second half, Coach Tanaka pointed at Johnny to sub in and play point guard. Playing point guard meant he'd be calling the plays. It was his job to make sure everyone was on the same page. The ball would be in his hands most of the time. This was his chance!

"Get in there and be a leader, Johnny," Coach Tanaka shouted.

Johnny dribbled the ball up the court and scanned the defence.

"Post-up, Donny! Xandro, stay in the corner!" Johnny barked.

Johnny dribbled hard to the hoop and made a neat pass to Donny, who made an easy basket. Johnny had run the play perfectly.

With Rex on the bench, Johnny controlled the flow of the game. He scored when he needed to and he set up his teammates to score. Johnny shouted orders at his teammates to sprint back on defence and to put pressure on their checks.

Toward the end of the third quarter, Donny grabbed a rebound and fired a bullet pass to Johnny. Johnny raced down the court. He shook one defender with a quick move and then took a jump shot.

SPLASH! The shot went in, hitting nothing but net.

ROAR! The crowd cheered.

Coach Tanaka subbed out Johnny to give him a rest and put Rex back in. As Johnny ran back to the bench, Coach Tanaka patted him on the back.

"Great job out there, Johnny!" Coach Tanaka said.

Dripping with sweat, Johnny took his seat on the bench. He felt as confident as he had ever before. He'd run the offence perfectly and the Knights had built a ten-point lead.

With Rex back in the game, the Knights continued to roll. But, Johnny noticed, it was mostly Rex being a one-man show.

Johnny watched as Rex put on a dazzling display. He made one defender fall over with a fake, ran past another using his speed and then he leaped over everyone to slam dunk the ball.

The crowd stood on their feet every time Rex had the ball. No one wanted to miss what he was going to do next. Johnny wished he could be out there showing his full talents. *They'd be cheering for me*, Johnny thought. There was so much more he could do. He'd worked on scoring moves all summer.

As soon as the game ended, Johnny felt sad. He felt he could have done more. Playing point guard had forced him to run plays and pass the ball. Meanwhile, Rex was free to put on a show.

★★★

Next, the Knights played against the Prince George Cougars. In the first half of the game, the Knights' starting point guard, Tristan Cane, went down, clutching his ankle. He had to be carried off the floor.

"You're going in at point," Coach Tanaka told Johnny. "Tristan might have ruptured his Achilles tendon."

Johnny jumped to his feet. He didn't want to play point guard and he felt bad for his teammate. But this was the chance to play the big minutes he'd been waiting for.

On the first possession, Johnny took the play from Coach Tanaka. The coach had chosen a play for Rex to score. Rex faked his man and then ran hard to the hoop. Johnny delivered a perfect pass to him.

Rex jumped high in the air and slam dunked the ball.

ROAR! The crowd went crazy. Rex flexed his muscles for the crowd.

Johnny dribbled the ball up the court on the next play. He made several fakes and moves on his defender. He was determined to make a spectacular play of his own.

"Run the play!" Coach Tanaka shouted.

Johnny ignored Coach Tanaka. He dribbled the ball between his legs, then made a move on his defender and forced a shot up to the hoop.

CLANG! The ball hit the side of the rim and bounced out of bounds.

Immediately, Coach Tanaka called Xandro to sub in for Johnny.

"That's unacceptable, Johnny. There's no place for that kind of selfish play," Coach Tanaka warned.

Johnny stormed to the bench. Selfish? Rex could do whatever he wanted. Why couldn't he? Johnny kicked a water bottle and sat down.

"You better fix that attitude, son!" Coach Tanaka shouted.

Xandro stepped on the court. The Cougars pressured Xandro all the way up the floor. Xandro lost the ball twice in a row.

"What the heck are you doing? You suck!" Rex shouted at Xandro.

"That's no way to talk to a teammate, Rex!" Coach Tanaka scolded.

It was clear that Rex ignored the warning. Coach Tanaka pointed to Johnny. Johnny jumped off the bench and ran to the score table to check in.

"Stay in control of your emotions out there, Johnny. Lead," Coach Tanaka ordered.

"I got it, Coach," Johnny insisted.

With two minutes left in the first half and his team up by six, Johnny dribbled the ball down the court and called out the play.

"Red!" Johnny yelled and pointed to Donny. Donny

ran up to Johnny's defender and blocked his path with his chest. Johnny used Donny's screen to get an open look at the hoop.

Johnny leaped into the air with a jump shot.

SWISH! The ball rippled through the netting. Johnny knew it was in from the moment it left his hands.

"Hit me next time, Hustle. I was open!" Rex shouted as Johnny ran back on defence.

"So was I!" Johnny shouted back.

Johnny tried to ignore Rex, but Rex kept telling him to pass the ball so he could score.

In the second half, Rex took over the game, scoring fifteen points in a row. Johnny knew he had to keep passing to Rex because Rex couldn't miss. The Knights ended up winning the game easily.

The Hill Academy Knights were off to the championship game of the tournament. Even though they had won, Johnny wasn't happy. He was doing what his coach had asked him to do, but he felt he could do more. He wanted to do more. He wanted to show everyone that he could do what Rex was doing.

"These guys can't see me!" Rex yelled as the team jogged onto the court for the final game against the Salmon Arm Ravens. "Nobody can stop the golden child!"

"Hey, Rex, how about you just play the game?!" Coach Tanaka yelled from the sideline.

Rex didn't stop boasting for the whole warm-up. "I'm going to light this gym up, baby," he gloated.

Johnny looked into the stands. Tracy and the rest of the girls had finished their games and were sitting in the stands. Suddenly, Rex ran up and chest-bumped him.

"Let's do this, Hustle! Look for me!" Rex shouted.

On the first possession of the game, the Ravens point guard pressured Johnny all the way up the floor. The Ravens player knocked the ball loose from Johnny and raced off on a breakaway.

"Get back, Johnny!" Coach Tanaka shouted.

Johnny sprinted after the Ravens point guard, but he knew he wasn't going to catch him.

Suddenly, a golden-brown blur roared past Johnny. It was Rex.

THUD! Rex leaped and blocked the Ravens player's shot against the backboard.

The ball fell right into Johnny's hands. Johnny raced up the court with the ball. He could hear Rex calling for it from his right side.

Johnny wanted to shoot, but he knew that Rex was wide open to score. Johnny made a beautiful no-look pass to Rex. Rex caught the ball and shot a jump shot from well beyond the three-point line.

SHWAP! The ball splashed through the netting.

The crowd went crazy. It became so loud in the gym, Johnny could barely hear anything. But he could hear Rex.

"I got your back, Hustle!" Rex shouted as they chest-bumped each other.

As the game went on, Johnny became more confident. Every time he or Rex scored, he could see Tracy and Amy jumping up and down in the stands.

At halftime, Coach Tanaka pulled the team together. They were up by ten points at 40–30.

"It's not the forty points I'm concerned about," Coach Tanaka scolded. "It's the thirty we've given up. Johnny, get back on defence."

Johnny nodded.

Coach Tanaka pointed to Rex. "Stop cherry picking and box your man out. He's gotten four offensive rebounds," Coach Tanaka said sternly.

Rex rolled his eyes.

"Are you listening to me, son?" Coach Tanaka shouted.

"Yeah, I got it, Coach," Rex said, without making eye contact. Then, in a whisper to Johnny, he complained, "I've got twenty points this game, and this guy is on me!"

"Okay, let's put the press on and break their spirits in the first four minutes," Coach Tanaka said, clapping his hands.

Johnny stole the ball three times. Rex had two huge dunks that sent the entire gym into an uproar. Johnny and Rex kept up the pressure on defence. They prevented the Ravens from scoring by deflecting passes and getting steals.

On offence, Johnny made sure everyone touched the basketball. Every time the defence made a mistake and left Rex open, Johnny found a way to get the ball to Rex to score.

The Hill Academy Knights went on to win the game 75–55.

"Way to go, Rex baby!" Johnny heard Tracy shout from the stands. Johnny's heart pounded in his chest. *Rex baby?*

On his way off the court, Johnny looked back and saw several scouts gathered around Rex, patting him on the back and shaking his hand.

"Great game, Johnny!" Coach Tanaka said as Johnny walked past.

"Yeah ... whatever," Johnny put his head down. He thought about how he had played. He'd played excellent defence. He'd run the offence. But he was unhappy. *I didn't put on a show*, Johnny thought to himself. *Not like Rex. It was Rex's show.* Johnny wished it had been his.

★★★

On the bus ride home, Rex made sure Johnny sat with him at the back of the bus. Amy and Tracy sat in the seats beside them. Half an hour into the bus ride, Tracy leaned over and tapped Johnny on the shoulder. Johnny's heart raced.

"Hey, Johnny Boy, you think you could trade seats

with me?" Tracy asked, batting her eyes and smiling.

Without saying a word, Johnny switched places so Tracy was beside Rex. It was the first time Tracy had ever spoken to him directly . . . and it was all about Rex.

As Rex gave Tracy the window seat, she asked, "Can I see your trophy?"

Rex pulled out the trophy. It was a golden basketball with the words *Most Valuable Player* written across it.

"Careful, it's heavy," Rex said as he handed the large trophy to Tracy.

"Kewl," Tracy breathed.

Johnny eyed the trophy in Tracy's hands. It was beautiful. All he had was a lousy medal around his neck that said *Champion*, just like everyone else on the team. Nobody was asking to see that. He wished the MVP trophy was his. He wished he was the one sitting beside Tracy Melrose.

Rex removed a deck of cards from his backpack. "Let's play cards, Hustle," Rex suggested.

"Deal," Johnny said.

Amy tapped him on the shoulder. "Do you mind if I sleep on your shoulder?" she asked.

"Uh, sure, if you want," Johnny replied.

Amy made herself comfortable leaning her head on his shoulder. "You played awesome today," she said as she closed her eyes.

"Thanks, Amy." Johnny smiled. At least someone noticed him.

In a few moments, everyone on the bus was fast asleep except Johnny and Rex. The two boys played cards in awkward silence while Amy and Tracy slept.

"Hey, Hustle, you think I'll make the NBA?" Rex whispered as he dealt a new hand.

Johnny looked up at Rex. Tracy was wrapped tight around Rex's arm. A feeling Johnny didn't recognize burned in his chest.

"I know I will. You? Maybe," Johnny whispered.

"Whatever. If you're there, I'm an all-star in the league," Rex boasted.

"Then I'm a Hall of Famer." Johnny countered.

"How do you figure? You're second best on this team." Rex never lost chance to needle Johnny.

"That's what you think." Johnny said. *Along with everyone else*, he thought.

Rex put the cards away and closed his eyes. "You kicked butt today, bro. I'll give you that. Every time I was half open, you found me. I wrecked shop on everyone today."

"Can I see that trophy?" Johnny asked.

Rex handed the trophy to Johnny and fell asleep.

Johnny hoisted the trophy above his head. It was heavy. Johnny's hands traced over the letters. *MVP*.

Johnny's mind replayed the games they had played. He had stepped up. All Rex did was shoot the ball every time he touched it.

Couldn't he be better than Rex?

4 BACK AT THE ACADEMY

As the school bus rolled up to the Hill Academy parking lot on Monday morning, Johnny felt nervous. The campus was crawling with students. Johnny wondered what they would say about the basketball team's glorious victory at the Penticton Classic. Winning was always a big deal at the Academy.

As Johnny jumped off the school bus, he spotted Xandro waiting for him. Johnny crept up behind Xandro, grabbed Xandro's pants by the pockets and pretended to pull them down.

"Hey!" Xandro jumped up, flailing his arms frantically.

"Easy, it's just me." Johnny giggled.

"So, Hustle, you big stud. You read about our squad?" Xandro asked.

"No." Johnny's heart skipped a beat.

"Oh, come on. It was in the newspaper this morning and all over Facebook and Twitter. Everyone's talking about how we killed it! We're ranked in the top ten!" Xandro said, giving Johnny a fist bump.

The boys walked to the entrance of the school. Johnny handed the security guard his backpack and walked through the metal detectors, his mind racing at the possibilities. He bit his lip. He wanted it all to be true more than anything. As he handed Johnny his backpack, the security guard said, "Nice job over the weekend."

Johnny turned and stared at Xandro. Xandro hadn't been joking.

As they walked through the halls toward their lockers, students stopped in the halls to meet and congratulate Johnny. Grade eight girls giggled, pointed and stared as they walked past. Guys they didn't know offered Johnny and Xandro high-fives.

"We run this school!" Xandro exclaimed.

Johnny could barely believe it. Everything had changed for him at Hill Academy. He had gone from being a faceless Grade Nine to being popular. But was he as popular as Rex?

BEEP! BEEP! BEEP! The warning bell went, signalling time for homeroom.

"You know what this means for us, Hustle?" Xandro said, beaming with excitement.

Johnny opened his locker. "What?"

"Big things. It's our time now," Xandro said, looking at his skinny arms. "Girls were, like, touching my arms. I might start doing biceps curls and get my flex on."

Xandro suddenly went silent. Johnny turned around to see Tracy and Amy walking toward them. Tracy was holding a folded newspaper and smiling.

Amy said, "Hey, John, nice write up in paper. Congrats." Johnny noticed that, every time she smiled, her green eyes sparkled.

"I haven't seen it yet. But thanks, Amy," Johnny replied.

"Hi, John Boy," Tracy said.

A lump formed in Johnny's throat and he could feel his armpits beginning to get wet with sweat. He kept telling himself to play it cool. He felt shakier than a bobble-head doll on a roller-coaster. He cleared his throat. "What's up, Tracy?" Johnny's voice cracked. He'd never heard it crack before. He swallowed hard and tried to remain calm.

"So, John-John, a few of us are meeting up to hang out at the pier. Do you want to come?" Tracy asked. The pier had become a popular hangout for students at the Academy. It was near the beach and the police never patrolled it during the day.

"John-John?" Xandro whispered. Johnny stuck his elbow in Xandro's side.

"Uh, sure. When are we going?" Johnny's voice cracked again.

"Right now, silly. But just you, Johnny." Tracy rolled her eyes at Xandro while applying pink lip gloss.

"Don't worry about it, Hustle. Catch you later,

man," Xandro said, after an awkward silence.

Xandro looked back as he walked away. Johnny shrugged his shoulders. He hoped Xandro understood that an invitation to hang out with Tracy Melrose had to be treated like a small miracle.

BEEP! BEEP! BEEP! The final buzzer for homeroom sounded through the hall.

"Well, catch you later, Johnny," Amy said, a strange look on her face.

"You're not coming?" Johnny asked.

"I have class," Amy said, and briskly walked away.

Johnny hesitated. They all had class. Johnny had stayed up late to finish his math homework. If he missed class, all that work would be a waste. He also had a quiz in science class that he had planned on acing. Tracy didn't seem to care about that as she placed her arm around his shoulder. Tracy smelled really good, like strawberry-and-vanilla cotton candy.

"You wanna hang out or what? We have to go now or we'll get busted," Tracy whispered. Her lips glanced against Johnny's ear and her chest rubbed against his shoulder.

Johnny's head was spinning. He knew if he was caught skipping class, it could cost him his spot on the basketball team. *But this is Tracy Melrose*, he thought. And he finally had his chance without Rex to interfere. Surely this was meant to be. He was running out of time to make a decision.

"So?" Tracy asked, clutching Johnny's arm.

As soon has her hand touched his bicep, Johnny flexed his arm. Johnny had to stop himself from shaking as he strained to hold the flex.

"Are we leaving or what?" Tracy asked again, impatiently.

School and basketball or Tracy? Johnny's mind raced. All he could smell was cotton candy.

Johnny shoved his backpack into his locker and elbowed it shut. *I'm popular now,* he thought, *and this is what the popular kids do.*

"Let's roll," Johnny said taking hold of Tracy's arm.

A whole hour passed as Johnny and Tracy walked hand-in-hand toward the pier. For a whole hour, Tracy hadn't stopped talking. Johnny was finding that paying attention to every word Tracy said was exhausting. As far as Johnny could tell, Tracy's world was all about shopping, makeup, gossip on Facebook, and her kitten, Jarvis.

As Tracy continued to talk, Johnny's mind drifted. He thought about how well things were going and how popular he had become. He thought about how the next day at basketball practice he would begin his mission to become the best player in the school — better than Rex. Johnny thought about his future. He pictured himself playing in the NCAA Tournament on national TV. He saw himself leading the Canadian National Team to Olympic gold. He could feel the weight of the NBA MVP trophy and the shake of the commissioner's hand. He imagined himself as a world champion with millions of adoring fans. If Tracy played her cards right, maybe he'd marry her.

"Are you listening to me?" Tracy asked, her hands on her hips.

Johnny snapped out of his daydream. He hadn't heard a single word. Johnny thought quickly.

"Yeah, sure. Uh, that's crazy," Johnny said, hoping for the best.

"I know, right? That's exactly what I said," Tracy said happily, taking hold of Johnny's arm again.

Then Tracy leaned over and kissed Johnny on the cheek. Johnny's face felt like it was on fire. His chest swelled. Every guy in his school could only dream of this.

"Can I see that paper, Tracy?" Johnny asked brimming with confidence. *They must have really praised me in the write up*, Johnny thought. *I did step up.*

Tracy handed Johnny the paper as they approached the pier. "You think you could get Rex to sign it for me?" she asked. Before Johnny could respond, Tracy ran off to join her friends.

"What?" Confused, Johnny unfolded the paper. Across the page, there was a large photo of Rex hoisting the MVP trophy. Johnny scanned the article. It mentioned him a few times, but the article was mostly about Rex and his show.

A scowl formed on Johnny's face, just as he saw Rex running over to meet him.

"What's up, bro? What are you doing down here?" Rex asked playfully.

Johnny shrugged his shoulders. Rex was probably surprised to see him there with all the cool kids.

"Have you seen this?" Johnny asked, handing the paper to Rex.

Rex barely looked at it before handing it back to Johnny. "Yeah. Raj brought it over to my house this morning."

Since when does Raj go to Rex's house? thought Johnny. Everyone in their neighbourhood knew Rajprit Singh. He had been a basketball star when Johnny and Rex were in elementary school. But he'd thrown it all away and ended up in juvenile hall.

"It's been crazy," Rex went on. "I've got so many people trying to interview me. It's whatever, though. You know, everyday thang."

Rex turned and punched Johnny in the arm. "You got some ink in there, too. I see you, Hustle."

"Yeah. It's whatever," Johnny lied, trying to sound as confident as Rex. It was anything but "whatever" to him.

"So, you rolling with Raj now?" Johnny asked.

"Nah, man, we're just cool. You're my boy, so I'll introduce you to the crew. But don't start talking about snitches, like before. Just be cool," Rex warned.

"You be cool. I stay cool," Johnny said.

Rex walked Johnny through the crowd, introducing

him to each group. Everyone knew Rex.

Tracy and a group of her friends ran up. "Hi, Rex!" Tracy said excitedly.

"Hey, Trace," Rex said. Tracy hugged Rex and kissed him on the cheek.

Johnny felt like he was going to be sick. Did Tracy Melrose just hand out kisses for fun?

"She wants you to sign this," Johnny said to Rex, slapping the paper into Rex's chest.

"Maybe later. C'mon, Hustle, let's go," Rex said. He shot Tracy a smile as they went.

Johnny noticed that some of the older kids hanging out at the pier were drinking alcohol. Others were smoking. Johnny followed Rex through the crowd toward a bunch of picnic tables where Rajprit and his gang were selling marijuana.

Rex walked right up to Raj and sat down beside him. Johnny held back. Raj's gang looked scary and Johnny didn't dare make eye contact with any of them.

"You know my boy Hustle, right?" Rex said to Raj.

"Your boy Hustle? He smoke or what?" Rajprit asked Rex.

Johnny looked at Rex. He felt completely out of his depth. Had Tracy just been using him to get closer to Rex? Why was Rex hanging out with Rajprit? What was Rex thinking? Skipping school was one thing, but doing drugs was completely out of the question. Wasn't Rex trying to be the best and make it to the NBA?

"Rex, we don't need this," Johnny said, knowing Rex would see his discomfort. "Let's bounce."

"I'm gonna stay here for a bit," replied Rex. "I'll catch up with you later, bro." He sounded casual, but he couldn't look Johnny in the eye.

Tracy and her friends took seats on the picnic table beside Rex.

Johnny didn't know what to say. His hands were trembling and his heart was breaking.

"In or out, rookie?" Raj asked, his muscular body towering over Johnny.

Johnny looked Raj in the eye and shook his head "Out," he said firmly.

As he walked away, Johnny could hear Tracy and her friends giggling. They were probably talking about how he had wimped out, but Johnny didn't care.

Johnny broke into a jog, then quickened his pace to a full sprint. He could feel tears welling in his eyes. He couldn't believe that Rex didn't have his back.

5 COMPETITIVE FIRE

Buzz! Johnny's alarm clock screamed at him from the bedside table. Groggily, Johnny batted a hand at the clock until he knocked it off the table.

Thud! The clock hit the floor and went silent.

Johnny lay in his bed, staring at the Lebron James and Kobe Bryant posters plastered to the ceiling and walls of his bedroom. One day he'd have his own poster, he thought. Johnny daydreamed about the action pose he would strike for the camera.

But if he was going to get to the pros, the first step was getting out of bed.

Johnny jumped up to begin his morning routine. He pumped out fifty push-ups and fifty sit-ups. After the last sit-up, Johnny popped up to his feet and walked to bathroom.

"Arrrgh!" Johnny grunted, straining to hold a flex in the mirror.

He was getting stronger, he was sure of it. Johnny flexed in the mirror in a variety of poses. He still wasn't as big or as strong as Rex, not yet.

Ten minutes later, Johnny was in the kitchen with a half-eaten piece of toast in his hand. Mrs. Huttle sang and danced in the kitchen as she watched Johnny eat. Even though she worked the night shift stocking shelves at Walmart, she always had breakfast ready for him every morning.

Johnny couldn't understand what she was singing about because she sang songs in her African language. He loved hearing his mother sing. She had a beautiful voice and Johnny imagined she was singing about happy things. The way she looked at him, Johnny often felt she was singing about him. Johnny finished his toast in one bite, grabbed his backpack and started toward the door. "Thanks, Mom!"

"Aren't you forgetting something Johnny?" Mrs. Huttle called after him.

Johnny ran back into the kitchen and snatched the cod-liver oil capsule, multi-vitamin, and vitamin C tablet from his mother's hand and threw them into his mouth. He washed them down in one gulp of water. Johnny handed the glass back to his mother and gave her a wet kiss on the cheek before sprinting down the driveway. In seconds, he was out of sight.

School passed by in a blur. Other students occasionally stopped him in the hall just to talk about basketball, but the buzz around the Academy was about Rex and how he was going to win the Provincial Championship for the Academy.

Johnny laced up his shoes in the locker room and prepared for practice. He couldn't stop thinking about what had happened at the pier. Every time he thought about how Tracy had been acting and how Rex had refused to stand by him, his fists clenched. Before leaving the locker room, Johnny took a deep breath to calm down.

Rex was already on the court, dunking and showing off.

Johnny grabbed a basketball and went to the other side of the gym to start his warm-up routine. He started to work on his free throws.

TWEET! TWEET! Two loud blasts erupted from Coach Tanaka's silver whistle. Coach Tanaka's short, sturdy figure waddled onto the court. His shiny, bald head sparkled as he scratched his silver beard.

"Today we're going to scrimmage and go through our offence. I want us clicking on all cylinders in time for the Cage Bowl Tournament," he announced.

Coach Tanaka split the boys into two teams. Each player called out who they were checking.

"I got Rex," Johnny barked.

"That's what you think," Rex said.

As soon as the scrimmage began, Rex was on the attack. Every time he caught the ball, he took it right at Johnny and scored. Each time Rex scored on him, Johnny grew more upset.

"You have to play better defence than that on this team, Johnny," Coach Tanaka shouted.

Johnny picked up his intensity. He wasn't going to let Rex dominate him this time. As Johnny began to increase his pressure, he started to notice that Rex wasn't his usual spectacular self. Rex was missing shots that he normally made. Johnny was able to steal the ball from him twice.

"That's better, Johnny. Good pressure," Coach Tanaka called.

"Lucky," Rex snorted as he jogged back on defence.

Johnny smiled. He knew there had been nothing lucky about it.

Rex and Johnny went back and forth at each other. Johnny became so focused on showing up Rex, he ignored the other players on his team. It was like he and Rex were playing one-on-one at their neighbourhood court.

The other players began to get frustrated, but neither Johnny nor Rex seemed to care.

"Ball! Ball! I'm open. Hit me, Xandro!" Johnny called, clapping his hands frantically.

Xandro kept dribbling the ball between his legs. "Fine, here!" Xandro said, finally giving in and passing to Johnny.

"Move the ball. Run the play!" Coach Tanaka yelled from the sidelines.

Johnny ignored him.

By the time Johnny caught the ball, Rex was all over him.

"You got nothing," Rex whispered, placing his forearm on Johnny's hip.

Johnny noticed what looked like pink lip gloss on Rex's cheek and some on his lips. Was it Tracy's?

Aggressively, Johnny drove to the hoop. Rex was right in front of him. Johnny flared his elbows as he drove through Rex, and one caught Rex in the face. Rex cupped his mouth and dropped to the ground. Johnny scored easily and slapped the glass backboard.

"And one!" Johnny shouted.

Rex popped back up and shoved Johnny hard to the ground. Johnny jumped back to his feet and, before he knew it, he and Rex were exchanging punches.

TWEET! TWEET! TWEET! Coach Tanaka and Donny ran in to separate Johnny and Rex.

"I've seen enough! This isn't the playground! Selfish and individual play, that's all I see out here. We can't win like this!" Coach Tanaka shouted at the top of his lungs.

"Hit the showers. Both of you are done for the day!" he yelled at Johnny and Rex. Then he saw the glint in Rex's eye. "Rex, don't you dare," Coach Tanaka warned.

DOOP! Rex toe-punted the basketball into the gym rafters.

"Come back here, Rex!" Coach Tanaka shouted as Rex stormed out of the gym.

Johnny touched his nose. It was bleeding, but he was too angry to care. He marched toward the locker-room, but Coach Tanaka blocked his path.

"What's gotten into you, Johnny?" Coach Tanaka

asked with a concerned look on his face.

Johnny shook his head. He felt wild. He couldn't think clearly. His face was throbbing and his eyes were watering.

Coach Tanaka placed his hands firmly on Johnny's shoulders. "Listen to me," he said sternly. "This game takes poise. It takes control. You lost your focus. If you do that as our point guard, you're only hurting the team."

"Rex started it!" Johnny snapped.

"Stop trying to compete with Rex and play your game!"

"I am playing my game!" Why was Rex the only one with a winning game?

"Control your emotions. You have to be a leader, not a follower. Now, go get cleaned up." Coach Tanaka said.

When Johnny got home that night, he went straight to his room without talking to anyone. He picked up a basketball and climbed into bed. He clutched the ball under his arm and covered himself with his blankets.

Johnny couldn't stop replaying in his mind what had happened at practice. It wasn't the first time he and Rex had got into a fight while playing basketball. But this had felt like it was about much more than basketball. Johnny thought about what had happened at the pier with Rajprit and Tracy. Maybe he elbowed Rex in the face on purpose.

Johnny felt terrible. He picked up his cell phone from the bedside table and dialled Rex's number.

"Yo," Rex responded on the line.

Johnny could hear yelling in the background and what sounded like Rex's mother crying. Probably another argument between Rex's mom and her boyfriend. Things were always crazy at Rex's house.

"Yo, man. It's me," Johnny said.

"Hey."

"Hey, man. I just wanted to say I'm sorry about today. It was my bad."

Johnny could hear a man's voice in the background shouting Rex's name angrily.

"It's nothing, man," Rex said. "I can't talk right now. I'll see you at school, okay?"

Johnny heard the click of the phone hanging up.

Johnny thought about what Coach Tanaka had said to him about his temper. He had learned in his neighbourhood that you never back down from anyone on the court. *Coach Tanaka doesn't understand*, Johnny thought. If he wanted to be the best, he had to show everyone he could beat the best. Johnny gripped the basketball in his hands.

The annual Cage Bowl Tournament at the Academy was coming up in two days. The Cage Bowl would be his chance to make his mark.

In the meantime, he would have to find ways to get better each day.

6 WINNER TAKES ALL

Both days since Johnny had fought Rex in practice, Johnny had doubled his morning routine of push-up and sit-ups.

Johnny thought nervously about the Cage Bowl Tournament. It would be his opportunity to show everyone that he was just as good as the best players in the province. *No, not as good. Better,* Johnny thought.

When Johnny arrived at the bus stop, Rex was waiting for him. Johnny noticed the welt underneath Rex's left eye.

"Decided to come to school today, huh?" Johnny said, trying to act casual.

Rex removed his hood. He had a fat lip too.

"Did you get whupped?" Johnny asked.

"Yeah, man. I got into with it my mom's boyfriend," Rex said.

Johnny shook his head. He couldn't imagine being hit that hard by a grown man.

When the bus pulled up, Rex climbed aboard and

dragged his feet to the back seats. Johnny followed him.

"You okay?" Johnny asked.

"Got anything to eat, Hustle?" Rex asked, ignoring the question.

Without stopping to think, Johnny handed Rex his lunch. Rex tore the plastic wrap off a peanut-butter and jelly sandwich and shoved half of it into his mouth. He sighed like he hadn't eaten for days.

"Hustle, why did you come to the pier?" Rex asked, chomping down the other sandwich and starting in on the apple.

The question caught Johnny off guard. He'd wanted to talk about it since it happened, but hadn't known how to bring it up.

"I was there with Tracy," Johnny snapped back.

"Oh, so you do like her."

"I didn't say that."

It still bothered Johnny that Rex hadn't backed him up, but he decided to drop it. He didn't want to let Rex bait him into getting into it, just so Rex could feel better about what was happening at home. But they could always talk about basketball.

"Just be ready to play tonight, Rex," Johnny said. "We play Whalley first and they're supposed to be *nice*."

"I'll drop 40 and we'll win. Just get me the rock and get out of my way, Hustle." Rex tilted his head back and closed his eyes.

Just get ME the rock, Johnny thought.

When they got to the Academy parking lot, Johnny could see Xandro waiting for him. Johnny started toward him, but Rex grabbed his arm.

A crooked look crept across Rex's face. Johnny could see the wheels turning inside his golden head.

"What's up?" Johnny asked.

A bunch of girls in a Jeep waved Rex over.

"You're hanging with me today. Come on," Rex said, pulling Johnny along.

"I'm not going to the pier," Johnny said.

"Forget the pier. Stop being a baby and let's roll," Rex snapped.

Xandro raised his hands in confusion. "Aren't you coming to class, Johnny?" he shouted across the parking lot.

Johnny looked back and forth between Xandro and Rex with the Jeep full of girls.

As they reached the Jeep, one of the girls yelled, "About time, Rex!"

"Who's your cute friend?" another one asked.

Johnny's heart raced. Did she mean him?

"That's my boy Hustle," Rex said.

Rex jumped into the back of the Jeep. A cute girl with long, curly, red hair, freckles, pink lipstick and a plaid skirt motioned to Johnny to join her in the front.

"Hi, I'm Nikki. What position do you play?" she asked.

Johnny cleared his throat. "P-point guard," Johnny said shakily.

"Cool. Jump in. I'll just sit on your lap. You can be my seatbelt, okay?" Nikki said, giggling.

Johnny smiled and thought about jumping into the front seat. *So this is what it's like to be Rex. A baller.*

Rex had an arm around each of two girls and winked at Johnny.

Suddenly, Nikki sparked up a joint. Johnny held his breath as the joint went past him. Johnny looked at Rex and angrily rolled his eyes.

"We have three games today," Johnny reminded Rex.

The girls in the Jeep giggled.

"Is your friend going to be okay?" one of the girls asked Rex.

"Yeah, don't worry about him. He's cool. Get in here, Hustle," Rex said.

Johnny shook his head. Things were far from cool. He wasn't going to be a part of Rex's adventure. Johnny had learned his lesson in Penticton when he almost got arrested, thanks to Rex. More distractions were the last things Johnny wanted before a big tournament.

Johnny thought about trying to convince Rex to stay. But why should he try to protect Rex?

"I'll catch up with you guys later," Johnny said and walked away from the Jeep.

When he glanced back, he saw Rex staring blankly

at him through the window of the smoke-filled Jeep as it peeled out of the parking lot.

★★★

WAMP! The horn sounded to signal the end of the warm-up, and the fans at Hill Academy rose to their feet to applaud their team. The Rogers Bombers, a gritty team from a town called Nelson, charged onto the court. Nelson was in the West Kootenay region of British Columbia, and the team had travelled far to play in the tournament. They were mountain kids and they looked ready to play the final game of the tournament.

The Academy had easily beat Whalley and then Maple Ridge earlier in the day. But it was no thanks to Rex. He was far from the 40 points he had promised to make. In fact, Johnny realized, Rex had missed more shots then he'd made, and had been making rookie mistakes.

The first two games had taken their toll on Johnny's legs, and they didn't feel fresh. Johnny ignored the pain in his legs and lined up beside Rex at the centre court. Donny won the tipoff, and the ball came right to Johnny. As soon as the ball landed in his hands, Johnny felt a surge of energy. Johnny drove to the hoop and made a crisp bounce pass to Rex. It should have been an easy basket. Rex missed the pass.

"Nice pass, Hustle," Rex shouted. "I'll get that next time!"

Johnny felt bad that he didn't stop Rex from going in the Jeep earlier. Whatever Rex had done that morning was making his game sloppy. When Rex looked bad, Johnny felt like it made his passes look bad. Rex wasn't getting open and their timing was completely off.

Johnny tried not to think about it. He couldn't worry about Rex. He started drawing the defence to himself by driving to the hoop. Every time defenders came to stop him, he passed it to an open teammate to score.

The Knights were leading 55–48, but they couldn't seem to finish the Bombers off. Rex kept taking bad shots and the Bombers kept making three-point shots to stay close in the game. The Bombers' shooters were on fire and didn't miss open shots.

Johnny needed to make a play to spark his team. He fixed his eyes on the Bombers player dribbling up the court. Johnny pressured him and knocked the ball loose.

"Cookies!" Xandro yelled from the bench as Johnny stole the ball and sprinted toward the hoop on a breakaway. Johnny jumped as high as he could and went for the slam dunk.

SNAP! The rim snapped down and the ball trickled into the hoop. It wasn't a clean slam dunk, but it was close enough.

The entire gym went crazy and the players on the Knights' bench stood up cheering.

It was first time Johnny had ever slam-dunked the basketball in a game. He stood under the hoop, flexing and yelling in jubilation.

The crowd erupted in applause. Johnny soaked it all in, waving his hands in the air to pump up the crowd.

"Johnny, stop showboating and get back on defence!" Coach Tanaka yelled.

As Johnny celebrated, his man sneaked down the court and scored.

Johnny turned and walked to the bench. He knew without being told that Coach Tanaka was subbing him out.

As Johnny reached the bench, Coach Tanaka looked at him and shook his head. "Your showboating just cost us two points," he said.

"My bad, Coach."

Johnny plopped down on the bench and tried to calm down. It had felt so good to be in the spotlight.

On the bench, Johnny could overhear Coach Tanaka talking sternly to Rex about being selfish on the court. Rex had scored 28 points, but many of his points came from one-on-one play and forced shots.

SWISH! Xandro hit a three-pointer and pointed to the crowd. The Knights were blowing out the Bombers.

Johnny stood up to cheer. "Atta kid, Xandro!" he shouted.

Rex made his way over and sat beside Johnny on the bench.

"I can't believe Coach benched me. I've got 28 points! He's tripping, you know, Hustle?" Rex said.

Without saying a word, Johnny got up and moved down the bench and sat beside Coach Tanaka. He'd had just about enough of Rex.

While Rex had just managed to fill up the scoring column, Johnny had played solid basketball. He scored 15 points, but also had twelve assists and five steals to go along with seven rebounds.

As the game ended, Donny walked over to where Johnny was sitting on the bench. He patted Johnny on the head.

"Way to play, Hustle. That was sick," Donny said.

Johnny slipped on his warm-up pants and sweater. He still wasn't satisfied. It was still Rex's show. When they announced Rex as the MVP of the tournament, Johnny felt like he'd just been punched in the stomach. Johnny sat in front of his locker while everyone showered, changed and left. He was too disappointed to move.

Xandro stormed back into the locker room.

"Johnny, let's go. There's a party going down on the west side. Let's get there before the cops shut it down!" Xandro yelled. "C'mon, everyone's already headed over!" Johnny began untying his shoelaces. He just wanted to go home and watch basketball highlights. But he thought about it some more. Maybe Tracy would be at the party.

In a few short moments, Johnny rushed out of the locker room. As he ran a pick through his hair, he searched the parking lot for Xandro.

Johnny saw Rex and Tracy sitting together in the back seat of a car at the back of the parking lot. Rajprit and his gang stood beside the car, smashing beer bottles against the asphalt. Rex hadn't invited him to join them. Rex hadn't even said goodbye when he left the locker room. Johnny watched from a distance as the car pulled away. Through the back window, Johnny saw Tracy lean over and kiss Rex.

Xandro jogged up. "You ready, Johnny?"

"I'm going home." Johnny didn't want to be around anyone, especially Tracy and Rex.

"Want a ride? I'll call my Mom, she'll be here in ten minutes. She'll drop you off," Xandro said.

"Don't worry about it. I'll walk,"

Johnny could barely contain his feelings. Did Rex have to win everything?

As Johnny walked home, he wondered what had happened to his friendship with Rex. He thought about how Rex was spending all his time with Raj, drinking and probably smoking drugs. He thought about how hard he had tried to be popular and win over Tracy Melrose. Trying to be popular only put him in bad situations. And it was Rex who ended up with Tracy. It hurt Johnny that Rex had taken the girl he wanted.

As Johnny walked through the night, he thought about how focused he had been on proving to everyone that he was a better ball player than Rex. It hadn't mattered. Rex still won all of the MVPs. It was Rex who would be ranked best player in the province.

Johnny thought about all the work he had put into playing basketball over the summer. Was he focusing on the wrong things? Was Coach Tanaka right? When he couldn't come up with any answers, he quickened his pace into a full sprint and ran all the way home.

7 TOO COOL FOR SCHOOL

CLANG! The sound of iron on metal echoed through-out the weight room. Johnny grunted as he placed the bench-press bar back down.

"Nice. That's more than you did yesterday," Xandro said, steadying the bar.

"Your turn," Johnny said, jumping to his feet.

"I don't lift weights, man. I'm still growing. I only work my biceps. For the ladies." Xandro flexed his arms.

Johnny smirked. "You haven't grown since the eighth grade!"

"Which means I'm due."

"Weights don't affect your height, man. That's a myth."

"Easy for you to say. I can't risk it."

Johnny moved to the squat machine and began loading it with 45-pound weights.

"You know we have practice in, like, twenty min-utes," Xandro reminded him.

"We play Tech next week. I have to be in top

form," Johnny said, placing the weight on his back. Johnny pumped out ten repetitions before taking a break. Vancouver Tech was Hill Academy's biggest rival in basketball. Beating them was all the Knights could think about.

"Hey, have you seen Rex?" Xandro asked.

"Nope. I don't think he's gone to class all week. But what else is new?" Johnny replied, stretching his calves.

"He hasn't been at practice either. You talk to him?"

"Nope." Johnny prepared to reload the weights.

"Ever since he won MVP and was ranked the best player in BC, he's been doing his own thing. I heard Coach is pissed." Xandro seemed concerned.

"Rex only cares about himself and his points."

"Yeah, but we need his points to win."

Johnny put on his practice jersey as he and Xandro made their way toward the gym.

The girls' team was just finishing up their practice with a scrimmage. Tracy was playing, but Johnny realized that she was one of the worst players on the floor.

Amy Stackhouse was putting on a show. Johnny waited on the sideline and watched. It was the first time he'd seen her play.

Johnny was impressed. He could see that Amy could score whenever she wanted. But instead of putting on a show scoring, Amy was doing all the work and setting up her teammates to score. Amy shouted instructions and made everyone on her team look better. Even though her teammates were scoring, it was Amy who was the star.

Johnny watched, amazed. It was just about the coolest thing he'd ever seen a girl do.

When the scrimmage finished, Amy ran over. "Hey, John, you guys have practice now?" she asked.

She was sweaty and her cheeks were a little flushed, but Johnny couldn't help but stare at her. There were butterflies in his stomach and, for a moment, he didn't know how to answer her question.

"Uh, yeah, we're just about to start," Johnny stammered, and his voice cracked.

He'd always known that Amy was pretty. Why was he so nervous around her all of a sudden?

"Cool, have a good one. I'll see you later, okay?" Amy said, touching Johnny's shoulder.

As soon as he felt the touch of Amy's hand, Johnny's heart started racing and his face grew hot. He wiped the sweat from his forehead, looking around to see if anyone could see how shaken he was. On the other side of the gym, Xandro was dancing, laughing, and pointing at him. He'd caught the whole thing.

Johnny jogged onto the court to begin his warm-up routine, going through the new drills he'd added since the Cage Bowl Tournament. After working up a good sweat, Johnny checked the clock on the wall. Practice should have started, but Coach Tanaka was nowhere in sight.

Johnny grabbed his water bottle and ran toward the locker room to fill it up. In the corridor outside, Coach Tanaka was standing in front of Rex with his arms crossed, holding several pieces of paper.

Johnny stopped short, not wanting to interrupt the meeting.

"It's bad enough that you think you can just show up to practice whenever you feel like," he heard Coach Tanaka say sadly. "But I just got an attendance report from the principal. It says you haven't been going to class at all. Your actions have given me no choice. I have to suspend you from the team."

"Suspend me? C'mon, Coach. We have Tech next week," Rex said, stepping past Coach Tanaka.

Rex walked right past Johnny and headed toward the court.

Coach Tanaka raced after Rex and grabbed him by the arm.

The entire team had gathered around to watch the confrontation.

"Rex, you have one option today. You can watch practice and support your teammates," said Coach Tanaka. "But you're not stepping on my court today, or against Tech, or against any other team until you start taking some responsibility for your actions."

"Don't you touch me!" Rex yelled, ripping his arm away.

"Watch your tone, son," Coach Tanaka warned.

"You guys can't win without me, Coach, and you know it!"

Coach Tanaka looked Rex over. Rex had a crazy look on his face and his eyes were bloodshot.

"Have you been doing drugs, son?" Coach Tanaka asked, grabbing Rex's hand and smelling his fingers.

"Leave me alone, man. You're not my father," Rex said, breaking free.

Johnny had never seen Rex out of control like that before. If it had been a few weeks earlier, Johnny would have stepped in. He would have said something to calm down Rex and help him get out of trouble. But if Rex didn't have Johnny's back, there was no reason for Johnny to help Rex. He kept silent.

"Rex, you're suspended from this team until further notice. And I'll be calling your mother. I'd like to speak with her as well," Coach Tanaka said with finality.

"You don't have to do that, and you don't have to suspend me. I quit! I don't need this!" Rex said angrily. He stormed out of the gym.

Coach Tanaka paused for a moment, seemingly in deep thought. He looked over the attendance record in his hand and crumpled it up. Then *TWEET!* Coach Tanaka blew hard on his whistle and the team rushed to him.

"Okay, guys," Coach Tanaka began. "I want everyone to understand that, to play on this team, to be a part of this program, you have to meet some expectations.

both on and off the court. And when you do not meet those expectations, there are consequences. That's how it is on this team, at this school and in life. Rex has failed to meet those expectations and has failed to take responsibility for his actions. The consequence is that he will be suspended from this team for the rest of the season. It's time for each and every one of you to step up your game. Bring it in for a cheer."

Johnny's heart jumped in his chest as the team huddled together. Johnny searched the faces of his teammates. They all looked shocked, except for Xandro.

Xandro was staring right at Johnny, mouthing a phrase over and over. Johnny read Xandro's lips. He was saying, "Step up."

8 A FRIEND IN NEED

Johnny boarded the school bus but, once again, Rex was nowhere in sight. For the past seven days, the entire school had been talking about Rex's suspension from the team. Johnny had ignored all of it. He hadn't even bothered to contact Rex.

The bus rumbled through the neighbourhood. It stopped in front of the playground basketball courts to pick up more kids. Johnny peered out the window. He could see Rex sitting on a picnic table near the court. He was with Raj and the rest of Raj's gang.

A part of Johnny wanted to tell Rex that hanging out with Raj wasn't a good idea. *But that's Rex's problem*, Johnny thought. Rex had deserted him and the team. Coach was right — Rex didn't deserve to share in what Johnny was sure would be the Knights' win against Tech later that day.

★★★

DING! DING! DING! As the buzzer sounded to end the school day, Johnny sprinted to his locker. He couldn't wait to get on the court against Tech.

As Johnny boarded the team van, he saw that Xandro had saved him seat.

"You ready to do this?" Xandro asked nervously.

Johnny nodded. He was nervous too, but felt ready.

Outside in the parking lot, the Hill Academy students were in a frenzy. There were dozens of cars and vans loaded with Knights fans heading for the game. They held signs saying things like "*Beat Tech*," and "*Go Knights*."

"What's going on out there?" Johnny asked.

Coach Tanaka leaned over and put his arm on Johnny's shoulder.

"Our rivalry with Tech goes back a long time," the coach explained. "Our path to the provincials always goes through Tech. And there's nothing worse than losing to Tech. I need you to be ready today, Johnny. I need you to focus."

Johnny nodded and put on his headphones. When the bus arrived on the Tech campus, the team was greeted by dozens of Tech fans. The Tech fans hurled insults and taunted them from the moment they got off the bus through their warm-up.

By the time warm-up was done, Johnny was fired up.

As soon as the game started, Tech put the full-court

press on the Knights. In just a few minutes, the Knights were down by 15 points.

Every time Johnny caught the ball, it seemed there were two defenders in his face slapping at it. Johnny kept trying to drive through the whole team, but ended up losing the ball out of bounds.

Tech was scoring whenever they wanted. Every time they scored, they showboated to the crowd.

The Knights were getting embarrassed by Tech. No one on the team seemed to have any fight in them. For a moment, Johnny wished Rex was on the court.

"Get open!" Johnny shouted at his teammates.

With the Tech gym rocking and the Knights on the ropes, Coach Tanaka called a timeout.

"What's the matter with you guys? We're playing scared out there!" Coach Tanaka shouted. "Johnny, get some control out there. Get us into a flow!"

"I'm trying. Nobody is moving!" Johnny said. The pressure was rattling him and he couldn't think straight. Johnny closed his eyes and tried to block out the crowd noise. He had to focus. His team needed him.

The Knights came out of the timeout with more purpose and less panic. Johnny led the charge by scoring two three-point jump shots. Johnny started passing to Donny. Donny picked up his play and started scoring.

By halftime, the Knights were down by just 10 points.

I have to take over this game — we won't win if I don't, Johnny thought. *This is my show.*

As the second half started, Johnny made moves on his defender, drove to the hoop and scored. After a Tech miss, Johnny took the ball the length of the court and scored again.

"This is our game!" Johnny yelled to his teammates.

Tech called timeout to slow down the momentum the Knights were starting to build.

After the timeout, Johnny found himself grappling with two defenders. Without Rex on the floor, Tech was able to focus on stopping Johnny. Johnny tried to dodge his defenders, but there were too many of them. Tech's defence was completely shutting down Johnny and the Knights.

Johnny was exhausted from trying to make every play. Tech was too good for him to do it alone.

Tech kept the pressure on Johnny, forcing him to lose the ball. A Tech player scooped up the ball and took it the length of the court to score.

As the horn sounded to end the third quarter, the Knights were losing by 18 points. On the bench, the team was turning against each other.

"Xandro, quit turning over the ball!" Donny snapped.

"Why don't you kick it out when you get doubled?" Xandro shouted back.

"Cool it!" Coach Tanaka shouted.

Johnny wiped the sweat from his brow. He took a deep breath and tried to catch his wind.

"Look, guys, it's not over," Johnny said when he could make himself heard. "Let's just get some stops and try to cut into this lead. We have to stick together."

Everyone on the bench went quiet until Donny stood up. "Hustle is right," he said. "We can come back on these guys."

"Grind it out — don't stop competing," Coach Tanaka instructed. "Johnny, break down the defence and pass the ball. Don't try to do too much."

The team huddled together and cheered before storming back out onto the court.

In the fourth quarter, the Knights battled back. Johnny did his best to pass the ball to his teammates when Tech double-teamed him, and Xandro and Donny were able to score off Johnny's passes.

The Knights played tougher on defence, making sure they challenged every shot Tech took.

With a little over a minute left in the game, the Knights were down by just 5 points, with the score at 75–70.

Johnny had the ball in his hands. He dribbled up the court and raised his fist in the air to call for a ball screen. Immediately, three defenders swarmed him. Johnny looked to his left and then to his right, but couldn't find a teammate open. Then, out of the corner of his eye, Johnny saw Donny open under the hoop. Johnny fired a bounce pass toward Donny. But the pass was too hard and Donny fumbled it out of bounds.

"No!" Johnny yelled.

With just seconds remaining, the Knights had to foul to try to get the ball back. But Tech made all their free throws.

When the final buzzer sounded, the Tech fans stormed onto the court.

The Knights lost the game 79–70.

Johnny put his head down and walked toward the locker room. It had been his show and he'd blown it. He thought it would feel good to play without Rex, but nothing seemed to be right.

Donny stopped Johnny just outside the locker room. "We can't beat this team without Rex," Donny said as they walked in together.

Johnny searched the faces of his teammates. Everyone seemed to be in agreement.

But there had to be a way without asking Rex to come back to the team. Johnny thought hard about the last play of the game. He should have found a way and taken the shot. He knew Rex would have taken the shot.

In the car on the way home, Johnny sat in the back seat, resting his arm on his father's tool box. His father worked as a carpenter there was always a thin layer of saw dust covering everything in the car. Johnny brushed saw dust off his shoes and stared out the window as his father drove.

Mr. Huttle reached into the back seat with his big, burly and blistered hand and tapped Johnny's knee. "You guys could have used Rex today."

"Yeah, right," Johnny whispered. He could feel himself getting upset.

"It's a shame what's happening to that boy. He's such a fine young man," Mrs. Huttle said.

Johnny rolled his eyes. "He deserves whatever he gets," Johnny snapped.

Mr. Huttle caught his son's eye through the rearview mirror. "Johnny, I don't want you talking like that. That's your friend," Mr Huttle said. "He doesn't have some of the advantages that you have."

Johnny shook his head in disbelief. As far as Johnny was concerned, Rex had all the advantages.

"Like what?" Johnny spat.

"Like a father, for one," Mr. Huttle said quietly.

Mrs. Huttle leaned over and picked a wood chip from Mr. Huttle's curly hair and another one from his beard. "And his mother has been having a really hard time lately," Mrs. Huttle added.

"Well, he's not my friend anymore," Johnny said.

"You know, Rex's mother called me today asking if you had seen Rex. I don't know what happened between you, but you two are supposed to be brothers. You're supposed to look out for each other," Mrs. Huttle said softly.

Johnny couldn't stay angry in the face of his parents'

logic. He'd been fired up to prove to everyone that he was as good as Rex, that he could run the show. He had thought that being in the spotlight would feel great.

Johnny wanted to tell his parents that Tracy, Rajprit and his gang had been more important to Rex than Johnny's friendship or the basketball team. He just couldn't bring himself to do it. Johnny didn't want to rat Rex out, and he felt awkward talking about girls he liked with his parents. But even though he was upset with Rex, and losing his best friend felt awful, losing basketball games made him feel worse.

Mr. Huttle adjusted his position in his seat and the whole car shook. His father was way too big for their little car.

"Son, a friend in need is a friend indeed. Do you understand me?" Mr. Huttle asked, staring at Johnny through the rearview mirror as they stopped at a light.

"I want you to call Rex when you get home and see if he's okay," Mrs. Huttle said.

"Sure, Mom," Johnny said. There was no point in arguing when both his parents were teaming up on him.

As soon as Johnny got home, he finished showering and then left the house. He wasn't going to call Rex. Why should he? Rex was the one who betrayed him. Anyhow, he knew exactly where he could find him.

Johnny jogged to the neighbourhood courts and found Rex shooting hoops. Rex saw Johnny walking up to the hoop, but didn't say a word.

Rex took a shot and swished it. Johnny grabbed the rebound and held the ball.

"You could have helped us today against Tech," Johnny said, firing the ball back to Rex.

"Yeah? Tell that to Coach Tanaka," Rex said.

POP! POP! A sound like rockets in the sky echoed through the air. The boys paused, their legs flexed, ready to take off running. The shots had come from far on the other side of the neighbourhood. The boys ignored it.

Rex dribbled the ball. Johnny suddenly noticed that Rex had fresh black eye.

"Your mom's boyfriend do that to you?" Johnny asked.

"I got into with it him again," Rex explained.

"You all right?"

"Just a little pissed off."

CLINK! Rex took another shot and made it. Again, Johnny grabbed the rebound.

"Things have been just so messed up lately," Rex said.

Johnny stood under the hoop. He wanted to yell at Rex for turning his back on him, but he kept his cool. His parents were right. Rex had his own problems to deal with.

"Look, man, I think the guys want you back on the team," Johnny grumbled.

"What about you?" Rex asked.

Johnny shrugged his shoulders. "I don't really care what you do."

Rex shot some more and Johnny rebounded for him. The awkward silence seemed to stretch on for hours.

Finally, Johnny decided it was time to leave. He'd said everything he'd had to say.

Johnny began making his way off the court, but stopped short. Anger welled in his belly. He couldn't leave without letting Rex know how he really felt.

"So you and your girlfriend Tracy are rolling with Raj's gang now, huh?" Johnny asked over his shoulder.

"Tracy isn't my girlfriend," Rex admitted. "Actually, since I got suspended, she and Raj have been pretty close." Rex shook his head.

Johnny couldn't believe it. Tracy had done the same thing to Rex as she had to him. She had used him to get close to Rex. Then she had used Rex to get close to Raj. "That is messed up," Johnny said.

"Yeah. Good thing you didn't go for her, Hustle. She probably would have done the same thing to you," Rex said.

Johnny walked off the court in deep thought. So Rex had had no idea what Johnny had been feeling for Tracy.

"Yeah, well, I guess I'll see you around," Johnny called from the street.

"Yeah, I guess," Rex replied.

9 ROLLING AGAIN

The Knights took the floor against the Westside Cougars. Since losing to Tech, they had lost another game to St. Mary's, a team they should have beaten easily.

Johnny was tired of losing. There was nothing he hated more than losing. He looked into the stands. There were hardly any people there. But knowing that no one would witness them lose didn't make it any better.

Johnny stood in front of his teammates.

"We need to get off to a good start! Come on, guys!" Johnny shouted.

But the Knights started off slowly. Johnny was doing his best to draw the defence and get open shots for his teammates. But none of them were going in.

The Cougars were hitting every shot they took.

Johnny huddled the team together.

"Let's grind this out, boys. We're not losing this game. Donny, post hard," Johnny ordered. "They can't guard you inside."

For most of the second half, Johnny passed the ball to Donny. Donny was much bigger than his check and was able to score easily.

Johnny's strategy of running the plays for Donny made it easier for the rest of the Knights' players to score. Johnny and Xandro combined to make five three-point shots in a row, and the Knights pulled ahead.

As Johnny dribbled out the remaining seconds on the clock, the Academy crowd rose to their feet to cheer.

WAMP! The horn sounded to end the game. The Knights had won 62–50.

Coach Tanaka grabbed Johnny by the shoulders. "All that matters is the people in your locker room. We won today because you put your teammates first. That's how you lead, son. That's how you become a winner," he said.

Johnny gazed up at the cheering fans. It was a packed house. Johnny was shocked at how many people had shown up for the game. He hadn't noticed as the stands filled up. For the entire second half, he'd actually forgotten that people were watching the game. The only thing he'd thought about was helping his team to win. Now if they could only beat Tech, they'd have a chance at a Provincial Championship.

★★★

Johnny sat in the locker room at Tech with his eyes closed and his head down, trying to visualize himself playing a perfect game. He could hear the roars of the rowdy Tech crowd outside.

The season had come down to this one-game play-off to go to the provincial finals. If they lost against Tech, it was all over. Johnny ran his hands through his already-twisted afro, trying to figure out how he was going to help his team get past Tech.

Coach Tanaka walked into the locker room and everyone took a seat. They looked shocked when they recognized who stood behind him. It was Rex.

It had been two weeks ago that Johnny had asked Rex to return to the team. Johnny hadn't heard from or seen Rex since. The team had figured Rex had given up on them. Johnny had felt the same.

"Gentlemen, Rex has something he wants to say to all of you. Go ahead, Rex," Coach Tanaka said, crossing his arms.

Rex stepped forward, his head down and his hands in his pockets. There were tears in his eyes.

"Uh, I just wanted to say that I know I let you guys down. I haven't been a good teammate. I do need you guys. I'm really sorry," Rex confessed.

Coach Tanaka stepped in front of Rex.

"Team," he said to them, "I'm told Rex has been attending class and making a real attempt to be a better student. I'm willing to give him a second chance, but only if you guys to decide you want him back on this team. Take a moment, we'll be outside." Coach Tanaka and Rex abruptly walked out of the locker room.

The locker room was dead silent. Johnny had expected the whole team to immediately jump up and down and welcome Rex back. But no one said anything.

Johnny looked at Donny. "I thought you wanted Rex back," Johnny said, breaking the silence.

"I did. But where's he been when we needed him? Even though we've lost a few games, we've played better as a team," Donny said.

One by one, each player on the team agreed with Donny's statement.

Johnny understood where Donny was coming from. Without Rex on the team hogging the ball, Donny was a focal point. His numbers had gone up, just like Johnny's. In fact, everyone's had. Still, Johnny couldn't believe how quickly they turned on Rex.

"What do you think, Hustle?" Donny asked. "He's your boy."

Johnny thought hard. As long as Johnny could remember, Rex had been his friend. As they were growing up, Rex had always used his age and strength to back up Johnny.

Then Johnny thought about how Rex didn't know that Johnny had really liked Tracy. He saw that Rex didn't go with Raj until Johnny had cut him out of his life. He thought about the problems Rex had been facing at home. He thought about what his father had said about a friend in need.

Johnny was surprised to realize that Rex needed him and the team as much as they needed him. He was even more surprised that Rex had admitted it. It was a brand new thought for Johnny: that Rex couldn't be a star unless he was part of a team who had his back.

"Rex is our teammate, right?" Johnny asked.

The other players nodded.

"We're supposed to stick together, right?" Johnny asked.

"He quit us, remember," Donny snapped.

"He made a mistake," Johnny corrected. "And he apologized. I forgive him."

Right away, Xandro said, "Me, too."

One by one, each player on the team nodded his head. But Donny held firm.

"Come on, Donny," said Johnny. "To beat Tech, to make it to the provincials, we need everyone."

Johnny could see that Donny was thinking as hard as Johnny had been. Finally, Donny said, "Yeah, you're right." Donny paused. "But I'm not taking any of his crap."

Johnny jumped to his feet. "Then let's do this. I'll go tell Coach."

Johnny ran into the hall, where Coach Tanaka and Rex were waiting.

"Have you guys made a decision?" Coach Tanaka asked.

"Yes, Coach. You always say the team that sticks

together, wins together. We all agreed that we want Rex back on the team," Johnny said.

Johnny extended a fist bump to Rex.

A smile crept across Rex's face.

"Go get suited up, Rex," Coach Tanaka said.

Rex dashed into the locker room. But Coach Tanaka held Johnny back.

"If you didn't see it before, this is proof now. You're the leader of this team, Johnny," he said. "And we can only go as far as you take us."

Johnny nodded.

Coach Tanaka placed Rex back in the starting lineup. Before the tipoff, the entire team huddled together. Johnny looked over at the excited faces of the team from Tech. Seeing Rex, the top player in the province, in the lineup, the Tech players began to fire themselves up.

"One!" Johnny yelled.

"Team!" The rest of the team shouted.

They stormed onto the court. The gym was more boisterous than ever.

As the game got underway, it felt weird for Johnny to have Rex back on the floor. Johnny was used to making all the one-on-one plays, but now Rex was always calling for the ball.

"Hit me, Hustle. I'm open." Rex clapped his hands.

Johnny looked away from Rex and passed the ball to Donny. Donny took it to the hoop.

Smack! Tech's super-sized centre blocked the shot.

He was so tall that even Donny had to look up to him.

Tech got energized by the play. They started hitting their shots and forcing steals.

Coach Tanaka called a timeout to try to slow Tech's momentum.

Johnny looked up at the scoreboard. They already were down 20–5. Johnny looked at the faces of his teammates and saw that they were rattled.

Tech was a physical, hard-nosed team. Their size and roughness intimidated all the Knights players except for Johnny and Rex. Growing up in their neighbourhood, Johnny and Rex had played against much bigger and tougher guys on the playground.

As Coach Tanaka went over the game plan, Rex grabbed Johnny by the arm.

"The guys are scared. You have to give me the ball," Rex whispered into Johnny's ear.

Out of the timeout, Johnny ran the play. He used a screen set by Rex and drove to the hoop hard. Tech sent two players to stop him. Sensing that Rex was cutting to the hoop, Johnny lobbed the ball up in the air toward the hoop.

Rex jumped. His feet left the ground, and he soared higher and higher.

Rex caught the ball and threw down a massive two-handed dunk right over Tech's centre. The Tech crowd went silent as the Hill Academy fans in the crowd rose to their feet, roaring in a frenzy.

With that, the momentum shifted toward the Knights. Johnny played fearlessly, using his speed and ball handling to dribble around and through the defence. But every time Rex flashed open, Johnny hesitated before delivering the pass.

"I'm open!" Rex yelled.

Rex was taking over Johnny's show. And Johnny didn't like it. *This time*, Johnny thought, *I'm not going to take it.*

Johnny ignored Rex and drove hard into the paint. He flipped a no-look bounce pass to Xandro, but the ball bounced off Xandro's hands and rolled out of bounds.

Rex yelled at Johnny, "C'mon, man. You saw me! I know you saw me!"

"Just get back on defence!" Johnny shouted.

Rex followed Johnny's order. He ran to guard the basketball. He pressured the Tech player with strong defence.

Johnny sneaked in behind the Tech player and knocked the ball loose. He raced down the court. The Tech centre waited for him under the hoop. This time, Johnny passed it off to Rex. Rex caught the ball and leaped into the air.

THUD! Rex slam dunked it again, right over the Tech centre.

"Yeah! Who wants what?!" Rex shouted at the Tech crowd.

By the end of the third quarter, Tech had taken the lead, 60–55.

Coach Tanaka walked up to where Johnny was standing on the court. "Johnny, you have to start working with Rex," he said and walked away.

In the fourth quarter, the Knights caught fire. On the first possession, Johnny hit a three-pointer. Rex hit another three-pointer on the next possession. Then Donny grabbed a rebound and put it back in while getting fouled. To cap off the run, Johnny made a bullet pass to Xandro. Xandro put his finger to his lips to shush the crowd as his own three-pointer went in.

The Knights were down 71–70 with just 15 seconds left. Johnny dribbled the ball up the court. He was determined to win the game.

"I'm open!" Rex shouted.

Johnny ignored Rex. This was Johnny's show. Coach Tanaka had said so. Johnny made a quick move on his defender and drove the ball to the hoop.

The Tech player guarding Rex ran to stop Johnny.

Without thinking, Johnny made a quick pass to Rex. Rex took a wide-open jump shot.

SWISH! The shot splashed through the net.

The Knights had taken the lead, 72–71.

The Tech crowd went dead silent.

The Knights crowd jumped up and down, cheering crazily.

The horn sounded to end the game.

Johnny pumped his fist in the air. They'd finally beaten their rivals.

After the game, Coach Tanaka huddled everyone together in the locker room.

"I'm proud of you guys. We came into a hostile environment and you stuck together," he said. "Now, you guys enjoy this win, but be smart and responsible. Hey!" he shouted. "We're off to provincials!"

Johnny cheered with his teammates.

Everyone ran to Rex and lifted him up on their shoulders, but Johnny stayed apart. He walked to his locker and began getting undressed. He was happy they had won. But he felt that he should have been the one to make the game-winning shot. Not Rex. Johnny.

If only he'd taken that shot.

10 WIN SOME, LOSE SOME

Rap! Rap! Johnny ignored the knocks on the door and continued to twist his hair in the bathroom mirror. He could feel Rex growing impatient.

"Hurry up in there, Princess!" Rex shouted from the other side of the door.

Johnny squirted cologne in the air and danced through the mist before opening the door.

"Geez, Hustle, you're like a girl, I swear," Rex complained.

"You can't rush perfection, man. Besides, the party doesn't start till we get there," Johnny said, popping the collar on his polo shirt.

"You mean, until *I* get there," Rex said proudly.

"What did you do, Hustle?" asked Xandro, pretending to gag. "Spray the whole bottle?"

"Don't hate the player, Xandro," Johnny said as he swaggered out of the bathroom.

Rex grabbed Johnny's arm. "Who are you trying to impress?" Rex asked.

"No one. Can I live, please?" Johnny said defensively.

"He's trying to impress Amy Stackhouse!" Xandro blurted out.

Johnny punched Xandro playfully in the stomach.

"What was that for?!" Xandro shouted.

"You know why!" Johnny said smiling.

"Amy Stackhouse, eh, Hustle?" Rex said smirking.

"Can we go already?" Johnny asked impatiently.

"Oh, so now you're rushing. Don't want keep your darling Amy waiting. You're whipped already!" Rex teased.

"Funny," Johnny laughed, shaking his head. He didn't take offense to Rex's ribbing, but he certainly didn't miss being teased like that when he and Rex were on the outs.

Before the boys could leave the house, Johnny's mother came out from the kitchen, her long braided hair tied in a colourful scarf.

"What time are you coming home?" Mrs. Huttle asked.

"Midnight," Johnny said sheepishly.

"Be home at eleven, and not a minute after!" Mr. Huttle's voice thundered from the living room.

"You heard your father," Mrs. Huttle said, disappearing back into the kitchen.

Johnny groaned in frustration.

"What was that, John?" Mr. Huttle bellowed from the living room.

"Nothing, Dad!" Johnny knew better than to argue with his father. "Let's go, guys."

"Man, your parents are strict, Hustle," Xandro said as they walked out.

"Like I don't know," Johnny said.

Rex looked Xandro up and down. Xandro couldn't stop looking around and checking behind him. He seemed freaked out by the shadowy figures hanging out on porches and sidewalks.

"Never been to the 'hood at night, Xandro?" Rex asked smiling.

When Xandro didn't answer, Johnny looked him over.

Every person they passed by on the dark streets made Xandro flinch.

"What, you scared or something, Xandro?" Johnny asked.

"Let's just hurry up and get on the bus," Xandro said.

"Yeah, he's scared all right." Rex was laughing.

Johnny joined in.

When the three boys arrived at the party, a throng of students rushed over to greet Rex and congratulate him on the big win for the Knights. It seemed the whole party had been waiting for Rex to arrive.

Several students greeted Johnny and Xandro, too. After beating Tech and winning a berth in the provincials, everyone on the team was being treated like heroes.

One student offered Johnny a beer, which he quickly turned down. Johnny noticed that Rex already had a beer in his hand. Johnny shook his head, and Rex seemed to notice it.

"I'm just having one," Rex said as he walked away with a group of girls.

"Whatever, guy," Johnny said, following behind.

Inside the townhouse, the music was blasting and people were dancing in the living room.

Xandro held his chest — he'd caught the rhythm of the music. He broke out into a dance routine. He started with the robot and then he cleared space to start break dancing.

Chants of "Go, Xandro" started.

Johnny clapped his hands and laughed as Xandro put on a show.

Johnny scanned the party as everyone watched Xandro dance and clown around. In one corner of the house, he could see Rajprit and his gang. Raj had his arm around Tracy.

Amy was in the kitchen, surrounded by her friends. So Johnny made his way to the kitchen.

Donny was also in the kitchen with some of the Academy's senior basketball players .

"There he is! There's the man!" Donny yelled as Johnny entered the kitchen. He ran up, flung an arm around Johnny and handed him a drink.

"What's in this?" Johnny asked skeptically.

"Just Coke, man. I know you don't drink," Donny said.

"Thanks, man," Johnny said.

"I gotta look out for my PG," Donny said, holding a beer.

"Go easy on that yourself, Donny," cautioned Johnny. "I may be your point guard, but I'm not carrying you to the provincials."

"Yeah, yeah. Come over here," Donny said, pulling Johnny along.

Donny introduced Johnny to the players from the senior boys' basketball team. They were guys that Johnny admired — guys that really ran the school. Some of them, like Trey Wilson, had already signed letters of intent to division-one schools. Trey was a point guard who could jump out of the gym and had a wicked jump shot. Everyone said that Trey would one day play in the NBA.

Trey stood in the kitchen with his hands in the pockets of his leather Knights jacket.

Johnny looked intently at Trey. The star point guard didn't seem to care about what was going on around him. He just stood there, leaning against the wall. It was like the world belonged to Trey, and he had no use for it. Johnny tried not to stare, but he couldn't stop looking at Trey. He was just so cool.

"Hey, Hustle, you met Trey yet?" Donny asked.

Johnny's heart skipped a beat.

"Yo, Trey, this is Johnny Huttle," Donny said.

Trey pulled his hands out of his jacket and extended one to Johnny to shake.

On Trey's finger, a massive Provincial Championship ring glittered.

"What's up, kid?" said Trey to Johnny. "I saw you play tonight. You're a real floor general out there, man. You all won that game because of you. Nice job beating Tech. Can't stand Tech," Trey added in a cool voice.

Johnny smiled and shook Trey's hand, which was like putting his hand in a vice grip.

"Thanks," Johnny said, barely able to contain his excitement.

Trey wrapped his big arm around Johnny's shoulders. "I like your game, kid. Let me know if you want to work out this summer," he said.

"Yeah. Okay!" Johnny said, beaming.

"All right, I'm out. Got a workout tomorrow. Peace. Peace," Trey said as he made his way out of the party.

Johnny's chest swelled. His mind raced. He couldn't believe Trey had been so nice to him. He was surprised to find that Trey's compliment changed the way Johnny was feeling about the game. All night, he'd felt upset about passing to Rex instead of taking the shot. But a star point guard saw that Johnny had been a leader through the game.

Johnny felt a gentle tap on his shoulder.

"Oh, hey, Amy," Johnny said. He hadn't noticed her walk up.

"Hi, Hustle," Amy said.

"Since when do you call me Hustle?" Johnny asked.

"That's what everyone calls you, right? Hustle-man!" Amy said, laughing.

"Now you're a comedian?" Johnny said.

Amy touched Johnny's hair and smiled. "I like it," she said.

Johnny stared at Amy. He remembered how amazed he had been with how Amy Stackhouse played basket-ball. She was a star because she made everyone else around her better. Johnny liked Amy, he knew he did, but he didn't know how to tell her.

"Wanna dance?" Johnny blurted out.

"Yeah, sure." Amy said.

Amy took Johnny by the hand and led him into the living room. Amy was a great dancer and Johnny did his best to keep up. When the songs turned slow, Amy moved in closer and Johnny placed his hands on her waist.

Amy was staring into his eyes. Johnny's heart was racing. He thought about kissing her.

Suddenly, students were bumping into Johnny and Amy. It was like there was an earthquake going on inside the house. Everyone was yelling and heading for the doors.

"What's happening?" Johnny let go of Amy's waist and looked around.

Rex was standing a few feet away. Johnny grabbed him by the arm.

"What's going on? Is it the cops?" Johnny asked.

"No, there's some guys outside from Tech calling out Raj's crew," Rex said.

The crowd parted as Raj and his crew made their way through the party. Raj stopped in front of Johnny and Rex.

"Let's go represent, boys!" Raj shouted.

Johnny looked at Rex.

"Forget it, Rex," Johnny whispered into Rex's ear. "It's not your fight."

There were cries of "Go get 'em, Hustle!" and "Handle your business, Rex!" from a few students.

"Come with me," Rex said, turning to Johnny.

Amy grabbed Johnny's hand.

"You don't have to follow the crowd," Amy said.

"You should really go home, Amy." He had to stick with Rex.

Johnny followed Rex outside.

A gang from Tech was hurling insults and smashing beer bottles against the sidewalk.

The Academy students kept egging on Raj and his gang to do something about the disrespect.

Johnny looked at Rex again and then at Rajprit, who was standing nearby. Johnny thought about what Amy had said to him. He remembered what had happened at the pier. Johnny could help Rex make the right decision this time.

"We don't have to do this. Come on, Rex," Johnny pleaded with his friend.

When Rex didn't respond, Johnny clenched his fists.

Rex looked at Johnny and then at Rajprit and his gang.

Rajprit and his gang were charging toward the Tech gang and the crowd was getting rowdy. Rex looked around at the faces of the people who were encouraging him to join in.

"Who cares what they think?" Johnny said.

Rex eyed Tracy cheering on the fight and calling Raj her warrior.

Rex turned to Johnny and smiled.

"You're right, Hustle. Let's bounce," Rex said.

Johnny and Rex turned and began walking away through the crowd.

Behind them, a brawl was breaking out. There were boys fighting everywhere in the street.

As Johnny made his way through the crowd, he felt two hands shove him in the back. He fell face down on the pavement. As he rolled over on his back, he saw a large boot heading toward his face. Johnny braced for the impact, but it never came.

CRACK! Rex punched Johnny's attacker so hard it sounded like a firecracker. Then Rex screamed and clutched his right hand.

Another boy from the Tech gang put Rex in a chokehold from behind.

Johnny jumped to his feet and tackled the other boy to the ground. Johnny gave the boy one punch to the stomach and one to the chin, and then he broke free.

WHOOP! WHOOP! Police sirens blasted through the air.

"My hand!" Rex screamed in pain.

Johnny jumped to his feet and grabbed Rex. "Let's go!" he yelled.

Suddenly, Johnny could feel his eyes burning. He looked around, but his vision was failing him.

"My eyes!" Rex shouted.

Everyone in the street began shielding their eyes as the police started filling the air with pepper spray. Through watering eyes, Johnny saw Rajprit being handcuffed.

"Rex! Go!" Johnny shouted.

Johnny and Rex ran as fast as they could. Though they could barely see, they knew the escape route. They darted through an alley, cut through some yards, and didn't stop running until they reached the boarded-up shelter where they always hid.

Johnny's face was covered in tears. His eyes stung like crazy.

Rex sat down in front of the shed, clutching his hand. Tears from the pepper spray dripped from his eyes. Johnny plopped down beside him. He reached for Rex's hand.

"Let me see it," Johnny said, squinting.

"Don't touch it." Rex grimaced.

Rex's right hand was swelling up like a balloon.

"We gotta get you to the hospital, man." Johnny helped Rex to his feet.

"Oh, so now you're a doctor," Rex said, forcing a smile onto his tear-stained face.

11 HUSTLE TIME

Early in the morning, the Hill Academy Knights bus drove onto a ferry. The ferry roared along the Pacific coast and over to Vancouver Island. It was rainy outside and cold. The boys stared out over the bow of the ferry.

The ocean was full of life. Ducks swam, seagulls swooped, and whales the size of buses spouted and leaped into the air. Schools of fish flashed about, and eagles dove after them. Johnny saw how every creature went about its business.

And the Knights' business was to play in the Provincial Championship. Johnny knew he should be focusing on helping the team win, but he couldn't stop thinking about Rex. They had left Rex in the hospital when the team had set off so early it was still dark. Johnny was getting ready to play the biggest games in his life and he wished Rex was there to have his back.

I should have had Rex's back, thought Johnny. Rex had got hurt protecting him. Johnny replayed the fight at the party over and over in his mind. But he still couldn't see how he could have kept Rex from getting hurt and the team from being shorthanded.

Everyone on the team was in a sombre mood as they drove to the Port Alberni gym. Again, they had to try to win without the top-ranked player in the province. They were playing the Hawks, a gritty team from small town of Trail in the mountainous interior of BC.

The Academy players couldn't shake their mood for the first half of play. There was no fight in the team. The Trail Hawks, though ranked much lower, were taking it to the Knights.

Johnny thought how much easier it was to play when Rex was on the floor with him. Determined to make up for Rex's absence, Johnny kept forcing shots and missing.

"Where's your head at, Johnny?" Coach Tanaka shouted as Johnny ran past the bench.

Xandro managed to hit two straight three-pointers at the end of the first half. The Knights headed into the locker room down 30–20.

The Knights sat in silence. Everyone had their heads down, waiting for Coach Tanaka to come in. Finally, Coach Tanaka stomped into the locker room. He didn't say a word, only pointed at Johnny. Johnny stood up and Coach Tanaka pulled him aside.

"You think it's your fault Rex isn't in uniform?" Coach said.

Johnny put his head down.

Coach Tanaka placed his hands firmly on Johnny's shoulders and looked him square in the eye. "How hard did you work this summer and this season to be the best you could be?" he asked.

"I worked my hardest, Coach," Johnny said shakily.

"I know it. I've seen it in your game. Are you going to let all of your practice go to waste?"

"No, Coach," Johnny said more steadily.

"Okay, then. I want you to go back in there and get your team ready to play. Do you understand that? This is your team, isn't it?" Coach Tanaka said firmly.

"Yes, Coach!" Johnny shouted.

Coach Tanaka left the locker room as purposefully as he had entered.

Johnny walked up to his teammates and looked each one of them in eye. "That's the worst half of basketball we've ever played, boys. It was like I was playing for the other team," he said.

Donny smirked. "Me, too," he said.

The rest of the team let out a nervous laugh.

"But, thanks to Xandro, we're only down by ten," Johnny said, patting Xandro on the back.

"We don't have Rex," Johnny continued, his voice rising to a shout. "We're not going to score every time. But we've won without Rex before. We got this. We put in the work. Come on, let's get it!"

The Knights jumped to their feet and huddled together.

"One!" Johnny yelled.

"Team!" the rest of the Knights shouted. Together, they stormed out of the locker room.

By the time the Knights reached the floor, the Hawks were already waiting. Donny inbounded the ball to Johnny. Johnny blew by his check and floated the ball into the hoop.

"Press!" Coach Tanaka shouted from the bench.

The Knights picked up, playing aggressively, full-court man-to-man. Johnny intercepted the ball from his check's hands and went in for another score.

"Let's go!" Johnny shouted.

The Knights were fired up and started clicking on all cylinders. They scored 15 straight points and completely shut down the Hawks offence.

They didn't look back until they'd clinched that first game of the finals, 82-60.

Back in the locker room after the game, Coach Tanaka grabbed Johnny by the shoulders. "You lead by example. Do you understand that?!" he said.

"Yes, Coach!" Johnny shouted before joining his teammates in celebration. When the Knights took the floor that evening against the Princeton Cougars, Johnny was ready.

In the first three offensive plays of the game, Johnny took three jump shots. *Swack! Swack! Swack!* All three shots found the bottom of the mesh. Johnny had come to see that when he was aggressive early in the game, it made the other team's defence focus on him. That made it easier for him to get his teammates chances to score.

Johnny looked to make a big defensive play. He knew that when his teammates saw him making effort plays, they tried to make them too, and their defence became strong.

Johnny read the eyes of his check. As his opponent tried to make a pass, Johnny jumped in the way of the throw, intercepting it. He took off on a partial breakaway.

But a Cougars defender pushed Johnny to prevent him from scoring. Still, Johnny didn't give up. While falling, he was able to switch the ball to his left hand in the air. From the awkward angle, he shot the ball toward the net. The crowd was hushed, watching the ball as it dropped into the basket.

"And one!" Johnny shouted triumphantly. Plus, the ref called the other team for the foul on Johnny, too!

Seeing there were twenty seconds left in the half, Johnny calmly ran the clock down. When it hit six seconds, he began his move. The Cougars had changed their game plan and sent more defenders to Johnny, hoping to stop him. But he spun out of the trap. He zipped a quick pass to Xandro. With a defender running at him, Xandro jumped. Seeming to hang up in the air, he shot for a three-pointer.

SWACK! Nothing but net.

As the buzzer sounded to end the half, Xandro and Johnny leaped at each other and chest bumped at centre court.

"You know I saw you, baby!" Johnny yelled.

Having built a twenty-point lead at halftime, the Knights went on to rout the Cougars, 72–56. Johnny finished with 30 points and Donny chipped in 26 points.

They were off to the final.

With the Knights still celebrating on the court, Xandro tapped Johnny on the shoulder and pointed to the stands.

"We play them," Xandro said.

A team dressed in black stood up in the front row: the Saint Thomas Dragons. They were the top-ranked team in the province. And they had the second-best player in the province, a Filipino point guard named Carlos Macapinlac. Everyone called him "Mac."

As the stands started to clear, Mac lingered. He stared down at Johnny as the rest of Dragons filed out of the gym.

★★★

The Knights team was quiet on bus ride to the final game of the Provincial Championship. Johnny couldn't tell if everyone was nervous or just really focused.

When they reached the locker room, they found

Rex there. He was in his uniform, his right hand wrapped in a soft cast.

Everyone on the team was in shock. Johnny's jaw dropped.

"Yes!" Xandro shouted and started dancing.

"Rex, man, you going to play?" Johnny asked.

"I wouldn't miss this, Hustle," Rex said.

"Can you play?" Donny asked.

"I can help," Rex replied. "I'd play even if I only had one arm."

"That's right," shouted Coach Tanaka. "Leave everything you've got on the floor, boys. Be proud of your efforts! Support your teammates! Play with no fear in your hearts! Let's go, Knights!"

The Knights charged out of the locker room and into the gym.

During warm-up, Johnny threw passes for Rex to catch.

"Ouch!" Rex shouted each time he tried to catch the ball.

"You sure you can play?" Johnny asked, worried.

"I'll do what I can. Worry about yourself, Hustle," Rex told him.

Johnny could tell that Rex's hand was too sore for him to be playing. He looked into Rex's eyes. He saw that Rex knew it was too soon to be back in the game. Rex was in severe pain, but he was still there to do whatever he could to help the team win.

Johnny patted Rex on the back, then looked up into the stands.

Amy was in there and blew Johnny a kiss. Then Johnny saw his parents in the first row, waving to him.

Bap! Bap! Bap! Mac bounced the ball so hard into the hardwood, it sounded like he was dribbling a bowling ball. He jogged over and tapped Rex on the shoulder.

"What's up Mac? Haven't seen you since I worked you over in club ball last summer," Rex said.

"Too bad you're injured. I was looking forward to schooling you. Who do you have now? Who's going to stop me? You can't stop me with that hand, King. I might go for 50 tonight." Mac boasted, dribbling the ball between his legs. "This is going to be easy."

"School me?" Rex replied. "Mac, you know better. We ain't worried about you. You ain't got nothing today. My boy Hustle's got you. Me and you? We'll settle up later, believe that."

"Whatever, yo," Mac said, looking Johnny up and down with pure disrespect in his eyes. "This kid? You've gotta be kidding me." Mac ran off to join his team.

"Cocky little punk, isn't he?" Rex said to Johnny.

"Heck, yeah," Johnny whispered. Johnny watched Mac warm up. He could feel his need to prove Mac wrong boiling up in his chest.

Throughout warm-up, Johnny couldn't stop thinking about Mac. In his mind, he saw again and again the dismissive way Mac had looked at him. By the time warm-up ended, Johnny was so fired up he had goosebumps.

The players took their places for the tipoff.

The crowd stood up.

Johnny lined up right beside Mac.

"I'm about to make it rain out here, rook. Hope you brought your umbrella," Mac whispered.

Johnny gritted his teeth. This was going to be a war.

The ref threw the ball into the air and the Dragons won the tipoff.

The ball came to Mac's hands and he ran by Johnny as if Johnny was standing still. Johnny gave chase.

Mac stopped just beyond the three-point line and pulled up for a jump shot. Johnny ran past Mac, hoping the shot wouldn't go in.

But he could do more than hope. Johnny raised his hand in Mac's face to distract him. Mac got the shot away, then flailed his arms and fell down to the ground, holding his face as if he'd be shot by a sniper.

Swack! Mac's three-point shot splashed through the netting.

The referee blew the whistle to call the foul on Johnny.

"I didn't touch him!" Johnny complained.

Mac smirked as he walked to the free-throw line. Johnny's "foul" meant Mac would get to shoot for a chance to make it a four-point play.

Swish! Mac made the free throw.

Johnny looked into the stands at the hundreds of cheering fans. Mac was like Rex; he played to shine, to make everyone else look ordinary. But Mac was also dirty. Johnny could live with losing to Rex because Rex was his friend. Mac was a rival. Johnny couldn't let Mac show him up in front of everyone. *Not today*, Johnny thought. *This is my time.*

Johnny raced up the court. Mac was pressuring him and holding him when the referee wasn't looking at him. Johnny couldn't shake the Cougars' star player.

Johnny called a play. But before the play could be run, Mac slapped Johnny's hand and knocked the ball away from him.

"Cookies!" Mac yelled as he raced after the loose ball.

"Foul, ref!" Johnny shouted.

Angrily, Johnny chased after Mac. By the time he caught up, Mac was already scoring.

With his one good hand, Rex inbounded the ball to Johnny.

"Let's go, Hustle! Pull it together!" Rex shouted.

Johnny grabbed the inbound pass and slapped the ball. Mac was pressuring him again, hacking him and slapping at the ball.

"Come on, ref, he's hacking me!" Johnny barked at the ref.

Frustrated, Johnny shoved Mac in the chest with his forearm.

Mac flopped backward to the ground, flailing his arms as if he'd been hit by a car. The referee blew the whistle. *Tweet!*

"Offensive foul!" the referee shouted.

Johnny slammed the ball to the ground.

TWEET! TWEET! The referee blew his whistle again.

"Technical foul!" The referee shouted and pointed at Johnny. With the added foul for unsportsmanlike conduct, Johnny was at risk of being fouled out of the game.

"Yeah! Get him out of here! Yeah!" Mac yelled.

Coach Tanaka slammed his clipboard into the ground. With Johnny racking up three quick fouls, Coach had to pull him out of the game. He calmly motioned for Xandro to sub in for Johnny.

Johnny walked to the bench over a mixed chorus of boos and cheers from the crowd.

12 A TIME TO SHINE

Johnny took a seat at the end of the bench.

"No focus. No poise. You're getting caught up in the wrong things. Wrong things, Johnny! How many times have I told you? How many?" Coach Tanaka barked at him.

This isn't the way it's supposed to go, thought Johnny. Just minutes into the final game for the Provincial Championship, Johnny was benched, Rex was playing injured, and the Dragons were breathing fire at the Knights. It was like some twisted fairy tale. As soon as Xandro came into the game to replace Johnny, Mac stole the ball easily. Mac dribbled up the floor and scored a three-pointer.

Coach Tanaka looked at Johnny and shook his head.

Johnny put his head down. He'd let his team down when they needed him the most. He didn't know what had come over him. How could Mac get under his skin like that on the basketball court? Mac was cocky, and he was very talented. But Johnny was used to playing hard against bigger, better players. What was it that made Johnny lose his control?

Johnny tried to refocus on the game.

Seizing the momentum, the Dragons set up a half-court trap and Xandro dribbled right into it. Mac stole the ball for another easy basket.

Coach Tanaka ran out onto the floor, yelling for a timeout.

The Dragons had opened the game scoring 12 straight points. The Knights were completely out of sorts.

Coach Tanaka huddled his team together.

"Okay, they just ate our lunch and we got punched in the mouth. What are you going to do, boys? Are we going to fold? Or are we going to fight back?" Coach Tanaka shouted.

"Fight!" Rex and Donny shouted back.

"Get the ball to Donny inside! Rex, be there to clean up the misses! For goodness sake, Xandro, take care of the basketball!" Coach Tanaka called as the Knights charged back out onto the court.

Feeling completely helpless, Johnny plopped back down on the bench.

For the rest of the first half, the Knights kept giving the ball to Donny. Donny was able to score. When he missed, Rex was there, soaring high above the rim to tip it in. It was about all Rex could do with his injured hand, but it was something.

Mac was having an amazing half for the Dragons. He kept hitting three-pointers from everywhere on the court.

When the horn sounded the end of the first half, the Knights were still in the game. Donny and Rex, with his one good hand, had kept the Knights from being blown away. But they were still trailing the Dragons, 45–30.

Johnny lagged behind his teammates as they walked out of the gym to the change room. He knew that feeling sorry for himself wouldn't help. But he wasn't playing either.

"Hustle!" Johnny turned around to see Rex jogging toward him. Johnny leaned against the wall in the hall.

"This is so messed up, man," Johnny complained. "These refs are giving them the championship."

"No, Hustle, you are," Rex said, punching Johnny in the chest.

"You saw those calls, man! If you even look at Mac, the ref is blowing the whistle. I was getting punked out there!" Johnny shouted.

"You want to know why I always beat you one-on-one?" Rex shouted back.

Oh, boy. Rex had picked the wrong time to remind him how much better he was than Johnny.

"What's that have to do with anything?" Johnny snapped.

"Hustle, I beat you because you always get angry or too fired up. Especially when people are watching.

Then you want to prove something instead of just playing your game. As soon as you do that, I know I have you right where I want you. I use your aggressiveness against you," Rex explained. "That's what Mac is doing to you out there."

Johnny thought about it. He had been wondering how Mac got him to make all the wrong moves. *Was that it? Was Rex right?*

"Why do you think I talk so much smack to you?" Rex asked, smiling.

"It gets me fired up and out of control," Johnny said, shaking his head.

"Exactly."

"That's so cheap."

"Hey, man, you play to win," Rex said, laughing.

"So how do I stop Mac?" Johnny asked.

"Forget about Mac. Get him out of your head. Worry about yourself. Control your energy. You can make him uncomfortable with your speed and how you jump. Get into his head and don't let him rattle you."

"Got it." Johnny nodded.

The whole season, Johnny had been concerned with competing with Rex and outshining him, when he should have been working with him.

It wasn't about putting on a one-man show. As point guard, Johnny had seen his own success when he put his teammates in positions to succeed. Losing his cool wasn't an option for winning.

"Now, let's bring this game back. I didn't come here lose," Rex said, interrupting Johnny's thoughts.

They walked into the locker room, where Coach Tanaka had huddled the team together.

"Boys, we're playing for more than ourselves out there. It's about our hard work, our dedication, our team. Look at what we've gone through to get here. We're only one half away. Do this for each other," Coach Tanaka said.

Johnny looked at Rex and nodded.

"Johnny, you're going back in at point guard to start the half. No more fouls." Coach Tanaka added.

Johnny stepped into the huddle and every player placed his hand in the middle. Johnny placed his hand on top of Rex's.

"Come on, Knights. Let's do this! One!" Johnny shouted.

"Team!" The rest of the team roared back.

As they charged out onto the court, Rex grabbed Johnny by the arm.

"First play, fake the drive and drop the trey piece on his head," Rex said.

Johnny nodded and smiled. Rex knew all the tricks. Rex wanted Johnny to shoot a challenged three-pointer in Mac's face. A player like Mac would see it as a sign of disrespect.

A week before, Rex would have been begging for the ball. Now he was calling the play for Johnny?

Johnny felt his confidence growing, knowing Rex believed in him.

For the first play of the third quarter, Johnny took his time dribbling up the court. Mac pressured him the whole way. Johnny made a quick move to drive and then pulled up for a three-point jump shot. The move caught Mac off-guard and caused him to slip and fall to the ground.

The crowd stood up, *ooohing* and *aahing*.

YAKUP! The shot went in. The ball splashed through the mesh.

Rex winked at Mac on his way to chest-bump Johnny.

Mac slammed the ball down.

Energized, the Knights began playing tough defence.

Mac came down the court and elbowed Johnny hard in the chest, trying to get him to react. The blow winded Johnny, and it hurt him to breathe. But the ref didn't catch it.

Johnny felt anger start to run through his body. But instead of retaliating, Johnny focused his anger into playing defence. He wasn't going to let Mac bait him into getting angry and hurting his team again.

Johnny was beginning to frustrate Mac with his defence. He was daring Mac to shoot, but Mac was hesitating.

Mac tried to shoot over Johnny. Johnny jumped high and blocked it.

Mac shoved Johnny in the back as they ran up the court. Johnny didn't react. He just kept running.

On four straight plays, the Knights passed the ball around until it found Xandro for a three-pointer. After the fourth three swished through the net, Xandro raised his hands to the crowd.

Over the roar of the crowd, Johnny could hear his mother shouting "Defence!" from the stands.

The Dragons' coach was forced to call a timeout to slow the Knights' momentum.

Steadily, the Knights climbed their way back into the game. The Dragons held only a 60–52 lead at the end of the third quarter.

In the fourth quarter, the two teams went back and forth, exchanging baskets. Johnny kept making spectacular passes to open teammates for scores and taking the ball himself when the defence wasn't ready for it. Johnny was diving on the ground for loose balls and helping his teammates grab rebounds.

With the Knights trailing 81–77 and one minute remaining, Coach Tanaka called a timeout. Coach Tanaka drew a play on his clipboard.

"Here's the play. Johnny, you come off these two ball screens. Xandro you set the first screen on Mac, then Donny you set the second screen and make sure you hit Mac to free Johnny up. Once you're free Johnny, either shoot it or look for Donny rolling to the hoop," Coach Tanaka said.

As the Knights walked out onto the court, Rex grabbed Johnny by the arm.

"Forget the screens and take it to the house," Rex whispered in his ear.

Johnny stared blankly at Rex. That wasn't the play.

"Trust me," Rex said.

Trust him? In a flash, Johnny thought about how Rex had made him sneak out in Penticton. He thought about Tracy and how Rex didn't have his back at the pier.

But then he remembered how Rex had come back to find him when he was lost in Penticton.

He remembered how Rex protected him when he was jumped by the Tech gang member.

He thought about how Rex had shown up for the final even though it hurt for him to play.

He thought about the good advice Rex had given him at half-time, and what it cost Rex to admit how he always got the better of Johnny.

Rex had Johnny's back.

"I trust you," Johnny nodded.

Johnny dribbled the ball up the court and waited for his teammates to get into position. Mac was pressuring him, trying to force him to use the screens. Johnny started toward the screen, but could see the Dragons defenders coming. He had to use Rex's plan.

Suddenly, Johnny wrapped the ball behind his back and drove to the hoop hard. The move caught everyone off-guard and Johnny had a clear path to the hoop.

Johnny took one dribble. Then he jumped as hard and as high as he could. He soared high above the rim and laid the ball in gently into the hoop.

The noise in the gym was deafening. The Knights had cut the lead down to 81–79.

Johnny barely heard the Dragons' coach call a timeout.

The fans were jumping so hard the gym was vibrating.

Johnny could hear Coach Tanaka telling them to press and foul if they didn't get the steal. But Rex's voice was also in his ear, hoarse and raspy from yelling.

Rex placed his hand firmly on Johnny's hip. "They're going to Mac. Get real close to him and tug his hip like this, real sneaky-like. When he cuts to the ball, I'll leave my man and jump in front him. You go for the steal. Just make sure you get it, or my man will have an easy one and this thing is over," Rex said, punching Johnny in the chest.

"I'll get it," Johnny promised.

"You better."

"Trust me."

Rex nodded.

The Knights stormed back out onto the court.

Johnny looked up at the clock. There were 17 seconds left, the Knights were down by two points, and the Dragons had the ball. They needed a miracle.

The Dragons ran their play. Mac tried to cut to the

ball. But Johnny tugged his hip firmly once and then quickly let go, just as Rex had shown him.

Rex left his man and jumped in front of Mac.

Amazingly, Mac dodged Rex.

Johnny arrived late and Mac caught the inbounds pass.

Rex's check was wide open at the other end of the court.

"No!" Rex shouted.

Before Mac could throw the pass, Johnny gave one last effort. He lunged and knocked the ball cleanly out of Mac's hands. Johnny had the ball.

Everyone in the gym stood up cheering crazily.

"Yes, Hustle!" Rex shouted.

Coach Tanaka was barking out a play. Johnny couldn't hear a word he was saying, but he could hear Rex.

"All you, Hustle! All you!" Rex shouted through cupped hands.

The seconds ticked down on the clock.

"You got nothing, kid," Mac taunted.

Johnny was counting the time down in his head. He'd practiced this moment countless times on the playground.

"10 . . . 9 . . . 8 . . ." Johnny began his move, faking dribble moves to the right and then to his left.

"7 . . . 6 . . . 5 . . ." Johnny spun right, then he spun left.

Mac jumped in front of Johnny to prevent him from going to the hoop.

4, 3 . . . Johnny had to decide. He could take the open jump shot that would tie the game or — Johnny dodged Mac and jumped backward behind the three-point line. He was going for the win.

2, 1 . . . Johnny leaped into the air and released the shot over Mac's outstretched hand.

Johnny fell down on his back, holding his follow-through.

SWACK! The ball swished through the net.

WAMP! The horn sounded to end the game with Knights up 82–81.

ROAR! The gym exploded into chaos and fans rushed the court.

Rex dove to the ground on top of Johnny. The two boys hugged as the rest of the Knights dog-piled on top of them.

At the bottom of the pile, Johnny could hear Rex's raspy voice yelling, "You did it, Hustle!"

"We did it!" Johnny shouted back.

★★★

During the awards ceremony, they announced Johnny's name as the tournament MVP and handed him a large, golden trophy.

The crowd cheered as Johnny hoisted the trophy high above his head.

Johnny traced his fingers over the three gold letters.

His time to shine had finally come.

When Johnny returned to the team, clutching the golden MVP trophy, Rex placed his casted arm around Johnny's shoulders. As the team posed for a picture, Rex pulled Johnny toward him.

"Next year, it's my show again," Rex whispered.

"Well, I'm going to the top floor, don't get left in the lobby," Johnny said with a smile.

ACKNOWLEDGEMENTS

Thank you to my father, Daniel, my mentor, and to my loving mother, Betty, for her prayers and her guidance. Also, to my brother, Sam, and sisters Phoebe and Grace, for your support. Thank you to my darling Adwoa, for encouraging and putting up with everything that is me.

Lastly, Kareem Johnson, my childhood companion, thank you for pushing me to be better each day than I was the day before. Indeed brother, iron sharpens iron.

CHECK OUT THESE OTHER BASKETBALL STORIES FROM LORIMER'S SPORTS STORIES SERIES:

Camp All-Star
by Michael Coldwell

Jeff's been invited to an elite basketball camp, and he's looking forward to some serious on-court action for two weeks straight — but Chip, his completely unserious new roommate, seems to have other ideas ...

Fast Break
by Michael Coldwell

Meeting people in a new town is hard. So when Jeff runs into a group of guys who love basketball as much as he does, he makes sure to stick with them when school starts. But at school, he finds out what they're really like ...

Free Throw
by Jacqueline Guest

When his mother remarries, suddenly everything changes for Matt: new school, new father, five annoying new sisters, even a smelly new dog. Worst of all, if he wants to play basketball again, he'll have to play with his old team's worst enemies.

Fadeaway
by Steven Barwin

Renna's the captain of her basketball team, and is known to run a tight ship. But then a new girl from a rival team joins. Suddenly, Renna's being left out and picked on by her own teammates. Can she face this bullying and win her team back before it goes too far?

Game Face
by Sylvia Gunnery

Jay's back in Rockets territory after playing for a rival team last year, and not everyone on the basketball team is welcoming him home. When Jay beats out former best friend and MVP Colin for team captain, the tension threatens to rip the team apart.

Home Court Advantage
by Sandra Diersch

Life as a foster child can be tough — so Debbie has learned to be tough back, both at home and on the court. But when a nice couple decides to adopt her, Debbie suddenly isn't so sure of herself — and her new teammates aren't so sure about her either.

Hoop Magic
by Eric Howling

Orlando O'Malley has had to overcome a lot to play basketball. He's the worst shooter on the Evergreen Eagles middle school team. He can barely dribble around a cone in practice. And he's certainly the shortest. But Orlando has two special talents: a winning personality and the ability to call play-by-play almost everything that is happening around him.